What the critics are saying:

LUCY'S DOUBLE DIAMONDS is definitely an erotic story at the top of its game. Ruby Storm has outdone herself with this. Minage and HOT. ~*Phyllis Ingram, Romance Junkies*

A lustful and compelling story...the epitome of every woman's secret fantasy. With well-developed characters and unbelievably erotic sex scenes, this book is a definite keeper. ~*Kathi, Fallen Angels*

...a must for any erotica fan. Filled with emotion, humor, and sizzling sex, this is one story that will have you panting throughout, and wishing for a sequel at the end. ~*Enya Adrian, Romance Reviews Today*

Discover for yourself why readers can't get enough of the multiple award-winning publisher Ellora's Cave. Whether you prefer e-books or paperbacks, be sure to visit EC on the web at www.ellorascave.com for an erotic reading experience that will leave you breathless.

www.ellorascave.com

LUCY'S DOUBLE DIAMONDS
An Ellora's Cave Publication, July 2004

Ellora's Cave Publishing, Inc.
PO Box 787
Hudson, OH 44236-0787

ISBN #1-4199-5002-9

ISBN MS Reader (LIT) ISBN # 1-84360-809-X
Other available formats (no ISBNs are assigned):
Adobe (PDF), Rocketbook (RB), Mobipocket (PRC) & HTML

Edited by *Raelene Gorlinsky.*
Cover art by *Scott Carpenter.*

LUCY'S DOUBLE DIAMONDS

Ruby Storm

Chapter One: The Wish

Lucy O'Malley dragged her book of guest checks from the bottom of her apron, tilted her chin, and fanned the slender length of her neck. A second later, her hand swatted out at a buzzing fly that continually bounced off the smooth skin of her perspiring forehead. She expelled an exasperated and tired sigh as she unfastened the top two buttons of her waitress uniform, allowing a small amount of heated air to enter between her round breasts. "When in hell is Frank going to fix the air conditioner? Man—it's been a week already."

Mavis Johnson, the elderly employee sharing the same shift, shuffled her rolling mass from the interior of the café's kitchen. Her dark eyebrows dipped over a pair of thick lenses when she eyed the long line of exposed cleavage that disappeared into the white uniform of her good friend. "You won't have to be worrying if the air conditioner is fixed or not. If Frank sees you sitting there with your feet up and your boobs hanging out for the next customer to see, you'll be sitting someplace hotter—that being the unemployment line."

"Oh, screw Frank," Lucy sighed with an airy wave of her hand. "We bust our asses for him in this two-bit burger joint while he's out on the golf course trying to impress everyone with his 'business acumen". Her green eyes swept upward to the clock hanging over the entrance; it was eleven o'clock. "I intend to fully enjoy this momentary lull before all hell breaks loose. In twenty minutes, the crotch of my pantyhose will be hanging to my knees as I'm running one plate after another to the lunchtime usuals. Hell, maybe I'll be lucky enough to trip; Worker's Compensation doesn't sound too bad about now."

Mavis plopped a beefy fist on her wide hip and shook her curly head. "You're getting a regular paycheck, Luce. Frank might try to work us to death, but he's never missed a pay period, now has he? And the tips in this place ain't too bad, neither."

Lucy dropped her feet to the floor from the chair on which they'd rested, plucked a napkin from a dented tin box, and wiped her brow. Lifting the thick auburn braid that hung down her back, she grabbed another napkin and dabbed at the nape of her neck. "Don't you ever wish for something more, Mavis? Wouldn't you like to just break free? I can't see myself working here forever. Shit—I need to find a man to take care of me." The young woman stared dreamily into space with a soft smile on her lips. "Someone who would make my toes curl when he made love to me." Her smile widened as she daydreamed out loud. "A big, tall, dark-haired man with muscles that don't quit, sexy bedroom eyes—someone who would walk on fire for me." Lucy's head swiveled in Mavis' direction. "Do you ever wish for that? Do you ever wonder if there is really a man like that out there somewhere?"

The older woman continued around the corner of the ice-cream counter and began to wipe the condensation from the freezer's exterior. Her sharp mind contemplated Lucy's first question. "I've made a decent living working here. Who in hell would take an old woman like me and train me for some other job? No one, that's who. Frank's been damn good to me over the years. I know I'll have a job here for as long as I need it."

Lucy eyed the longtime employee as the woman moved along the back side of the counter, straightening salt and pepper shakers as she walked. *I bet he's been more than good to you.* She considered Mavis' words for a second. The woman never maligned their flamboyant employer. "Can I ask you something, Mavis?"

"Yeah, sure, you know you can ask me anything."

"Have you ever done it with Frank?"

Mavis spun where she stood and stared across the counter at the younger woman. "Done what?"

"Oh, don't be coy. Have you and Frank ever screwed? You know—fucked around a little?"

Mavis gasped, and then laughed a big booming laugh that Lucy swore came from the bottom of her bulging stomach.

The older woman shook her head. "The way you young people talk nowadays."

Now it was Lucy's turn to burst out laughing. "What do you mean?" Tossing her thick braid with a nod of her chin, she straightened on the chair and waved her hand to garner Mavis' attention. "Okay, does this sound familiar?" She cleared her throat and, in her best Mavis imitation, she giggled out, "Luccceee? Order up! Get in here! These fucking fries are getting fucking cold!"

Mavis belted out another laugh, shook her head again, and wiped the wetness from her eyes when Lucy tossed her a dry napkin. "Girl, you crack me up. Come on and help me. We'd better be ready for the rush."

"I can hear Pete banging around in the kitchen. He's got everything under control. You're ignoring me, Mavis. 'Fess up and humor me. Have you and Frank ever done the 'wild thing'? You always stick up for him no matter what." Lucy crossed her arms beneath her breasts and lifted a stubborn chin. "I won't quit bugging you until you give me a straight answer."

Mavis eyed Lucy over the rim of her glasses. "Christ, you're persistent. All right. You want to know the juicy details?"

The younger woman clapped her hands together with anticipated glee, leapt from her chair in the forgotten heat, and straddled a stool as Mavis rounded the corner of the counter again. Lucy waited breathlessly until Mavis sat beside her.

"I took to that son of a bitch the first two months I worked here," the robust woman breathed out quietly.

"Why are we whispering?" Lucy leaned forward to hear the answer.

Mavis glanced over her shoulder before meeting the young woman's gaze once more. Her thick eyebrows danced above her bright eyes. "Because that bucktoothed Pete in the kitchen has been after me for years. I told him I was a lesbian so he'd leave me alone. Kept the pressure off so I could play slap and tickle with Frank when Pete wasn't lookin'."

Lucy's hand slapped across her mouth to keep the giggles at bay. Finally getting a hold of herself, she leaned in closer. "I *knew* it!" she hissed. "Frank does have a soft spot for you. I can see it in his eyes when he's sashaying around here like a big peacock. And you—" she pointed a slim finger in the air, " — well, you run around with pink cheeks like a teenage girl!"

"Well, honey, I may be carrying an extra seventy pounds on these hips, but Frank always says, 'the bigger the cushion, the better the pushin'!'"

"Mavis!" Lucy screeched hysterically.

The older woman resettled her bulk on the stool with a smile creasing her face. "That Frank is something else. He's got a sense of humor that no one sees much but me. Hell, I remember the time when he said he was going to roll me in the flour bin and screw the first wet spot he found!"

Lucy lost it. It wasn't long before the two were mopping their cheeks again as Mavis struggled to finish her story.

"Hell…" Mavis squeaked between tears, "I tried more than once to tell him my ass was too big to stuff in the flour bin — that it would be better if he just reached in with his hands and threw the damn stuff at me!"

Their snorts of hilarity soon brought Pete through the swinging doors that led into the kitchen.

"What's going on out here? You two don't look like you're getting ready for the noon rush."

He appeared before them, his big front teeth resting over his bottom lip and flour covering his hands and upper arms. The image made the woman fall against each other in another bout of hysterics.

Knowing that for some reason he was the butt of their merriment, Pete turned on his heel and slammed back into the kitchen.

The old rusted bell tinkled above the door as the first lunchtime customer arrived. Mavis glanced over her shoulder and bounced surprisingly to her feet, despite her girth. As she moved to fetch a clean coffee cup, Lucy hurriedly covered her exposed breasts. The last button had just slid through the small hole hiding beneath the rounded collar of her uniform when she swiveled on the stool to greet the first patron.

Lucy's jaw gaped open. It was all she could do to snap her mouth shut before the pesky fly found its way past her lips and into her mouth.

Before her stood the man of her dreams. He was tall—at least six foot three inches—and he had the most wonderfully wavy dark hair. A white t-shirt stretched over a massive chest, across a flat belly, and into a pair of faded jeans. One bulging, tanned arm hung at his side as the hand of the other clutched a faded blue shirt. But it was his eyes—the bedroom eyes she had just wished for—that completely stunned her. They were as blue as a cloudless afternoon sky, twinkling below arched brows that were neither too bushy nor too sparse. Lucy's heart hammered in her chest.

"Hi." His azure gaze assessed the empty café in one quick scan. "You're open for business, aren't you? Someone told me this place puts out a great burger."

Lucy simply stared.

What the hell, is she deaf? The guy tried again. "Are you open?"

Lucy gathered her wits about her, cleared her throat, and tried to appear calm. "As a matter of fact, we are." She forced a composed smile on her lips, hoped she would make a good impression on the hunk, caught her heel on the rung of the stool, and pitched forward. A split second later, she was sprawled on the floor at his feet with her uniform wrapped up around her thighs. When she rolled quickly onto her butt, the motion popped her top button. Lucy watched unbelievingly as the white plastic fastener spun through the air and skidded to a halt between his feet.

He jumped forward to assist her to her feet, concern darkening his sexy eyes. "Hey, are you all right?" He couldn't help, though, but take in the line of her firm thigh as he bent forward and grabbed her elbow — or the line of her cleavage that peeked above another button that threatened to leap at him.

The red flush of embarrassment extended from Lucy's cheeks and down into the stark white of her slightly opened dress. She prayed for a hole to open in the floor so she could drop in and find a place to hide.

The man never even noticed her embarrassment. As his gaze swept downward, he only wished the second button hiding her breasts would pop.

His warm hand wrapped around her tiny one and before she knew it, Lucy was hauled to her feet. Sparks of fire leapt from the skin contact where he touched her.

"Did you hurt yourself?"

She still didn't answer him.

"I know you can talk because just before you executed that header, you were telling me this place was open for business." His gaze followed her hand as she straightened the nametag on her heaving chest. Forcing his eyes back to meet her emerald green ones that sparkled with embarrassed tears, he let go of the shaking fingers he still held. "Your tag says 'Lucy'. Okay, Lucy, you've got to answer me that you didn't hurt yourself. I don't think you hit your head, did you?"

She swallowed. "I'm fine," she squeaked.

"What?"

Lucy straightened her uniform around her hips. "I said I'm fine."

"Aha! You can still talk!" He studied her still red cheeks. "Don't be embarrassed. You're not the first woman to throw herself at my feet."

The petite redhead lifted her chin. Instant anger blazed in her eyes. "I wasn't *throwing* myself at your feet."

He lifted his hands before him. "Just kidding. Don't get mad. I was just trying to get your mind off the fall. You sure you're okay?"

One more look into his blue eyes and Lucy melted. Her chin bobbed a silent yes. "Thank you for your help. I'm sorry, sir, if I snapped at you. I feel pretty foolish."

"Well don't—and don't call me 'sir'. Makes me feel like an old man. My name's Matt. Do you think I could get something to eat? I've got to get back to work soon."

"Oh, sure! Take a seat, and I'll get you a menu."

They both moved at the same time. Lucy bounced off his hard chest, having misjudged where he was going to sit.

Matt's lungs constricted when her breasts brushed across his lower chest.

Lucy giggled nervously and peeked up at him beneath thick lashes. "Oops, sorry." She skirted his big body, grabbed a menu, placed it on the counter before him, and then ducked into the kitchen.

Mavis shook her head when Lucy dropped onto a small chair by the back door. She watched the young woman reposition the floor fan so it would blow toward her, presumably to help cool her hot cheeks. "Damn good thing we're not busy. What the hell happened? One minute you were on the stool, and the next hugging the floor."

Lucy dropped her face into her upturned palms. "Oh, my God... I've never been so embarrassed in my life. He must think I'm a real piece of work."

"I'm sure he does."

Lucy's muffled groan met her ears.

"But not the way you think. You should have seen the look on his face. Lucy, it's your guy. He's exactly what you were wishing for fifteen minutes ago."

"Don't be silly. After my little stumbling act, then almost knocking him on his ass a minute later, I'm sure he thinks I'm a menace to society." Her head came up. "Go get his order, Mavis. I can't go back out there."

"The hell you can't. Six more customers just came in. Besides, you've got the counter today. Now, paste a smile on those gorgeous lips of yours and get out there. Maybe he'll ask you for your phone number."

"Ma-a-v-v-i-i-s..." Lucy whined.

"Move, young lady! The place is filling up." Mavis turned and hurried out the swinging doors.

Lucy sighed heavily as she stood, squared her slim shoulders, and followed the older woman into the dining room.

Matt glanced up from the menu when she walked behind the counter.

"Are you ready to order?"

His eyes scanned her from head to toe, and then they widened slightly. *I'd like to order you!* "Ah, yeah. I'll have a California burger and fries."

Lucy scribbled the order on her pad without looking at him. "Anything to drink?"

"Just water—lots of ice. It's a hot one out there today."

She glanced up, and her breath caught in her throat. Matt was staring at her breasts. Lucy spun and raced back into the kitchen.

She ran orders for the next ten minutes. In between, she got Matt his water and nearly tipped the glass over when she set it down on the counter. He was quick enough to catch it before the ice spilled onto his lap. His chuckle caused her cheeks to flame again as she headed for the kitchen to retrieve a daily special.

Pete had just set a filled plate under the heat lamp. Lucy grabbed it, accidentally shoved her thumb into a pile of hot mashed potatoes, and watched in horror when the dish fell to the floor and shattered into a hundred pieces.

"Christ Almighty! Slow down, Lucy!" Pete hollered as he yanked another clean plate and began to fill it with the same order.

Lucy ran to the sink and shoved her hand under a cold stream of water. Matt had her in a tizzy! Her breasts felt as hot as her burned thumb. She had seen him checking out her chest and was positive that he knew he'd been caught doing it—and didn't seem to mind one bit. Most of the men who came in did the same thing, but all she wanted to do was cuff them alongside the head. Not this guy, though.

"Lucy. Order's up. Here's your California and fries, too."

She sighed, shut off the faucet, and wiped her hands on a towel. Being very careful, she picked up both plates and headed for the swinging doors. To her surprise, Mavis stood before Matt, laughing like the two were old friends. Seeing Lucy, the older woman motioned her over. Lucy dropped off the special with a customer at the end of the counter, and then approached her coworker.

"Lucy, I just about dropped my drawers when Matt here said hello. I haven't seen him in so many years that I nearly didn't recognize him. He's one of the Diamond boys. His family used to live down the street from me! The last time I saw him was when he was twelve. This boy's got a memory that don't quit and recognized me right off!"

Lucy smiled as she carefully set Matt's order on the counter. "So, you used to be a hometown boy?"

He grabbed the ketchup and squirted a dollop next to the fries. "Yup. Just moved back last month when the construction company I work for got the bid to remodel the high school. I decided to rent a place in town for a year since I'll be here that long."

Mavis squinted, deep in thought for a moment. "Hell, it's been nearly twenty years since your family left."

"Eighteen to be exact."

Mavis refilled his water glass. "So, did you bring your wife and kids with you?"

Matt shook his head. "Don't have either. Just been too busy working."

"Order's up, Lucy." Pete's voice echoed from the kitchen.

The flustered young woman turned and disappeared into the kitchen.

Matt watched the sway of her hips vanish as the swinging door nearly hit her in her ass.

Mavis was quick to pick up on his glance. "Cute gal, hey? She's not from Colby. Moved into town three years ago from somewhere over by Morton. Has no family. She was an only child and both her ma and pa have since passed away. I sorta took her under my wing. Her name is Lucy O'Malley and as Irish in her looks as they come. Spends her time working and fixing up Norm Johnson's old place. The homestead was near to the point of being condemned, and she picked it up for a song. Hard worker, that one. Don't think she's seeing anyone in particular, neither." She waited to see if the man readying his lunch would pick up on her obvious hint.

Matt wasn't going to bite. He simply chewed thoughtfully on his burger when Pete yelled for Mavis a second later.

Twenty minutes passed. Matt couldn't help but to secretly watch Lucy as she waited on customers and ran back and forth between the dining room and the kitchen. By the time she plopped his bill on the counter beside his empty plate, he had argued with himself as to how he would ask if she'd like to see a movie or go to dinner with him. There was something about this woman that had him on fire.

Only a month before, he'd sworn to himself that he wasn't going to get involved with anyone. He had managed to extricate himself from a four-year relationship with a clinging woman a state away and was going to stay clear of the ladies for a while. Hence, one of the reasons he put himself on the job in his old hometown.

But this redheaded, green-eyed petite waitress was giving him a hard-on without even trying. Her breasts were large, her skin milky, and he had seen the firmness of her thighs when she was sprawled across the floor. It wasn't hard to imagine that the rest of her body was just as toned. His jeans stretched a little tighter across his groin, and Matt wiggled on the stool. He hadn't had sex for three months and it was starting to wear on him. He wondered if she was up for a little fun.

Matt glanced up with a smile. "I haven't made any connections with any of my old friends since I've been back. Mavis happened to mention that you're not seeing anyone." He stood, casually holding his denim shirt in front of him with one hand and pulled his wallet from his back pocket with the other. He counted through some bills inside the worn leather, not realizing his shirt had slid to one side.

Lucy's stomach quivered at the sight of a furred, taut belly peeking out from beneath the t-shirt that had come loose from his waist. Her gaze dropped to the bulge at his crotch.

He tossed some bills onto the counter. "How would you like to take in a movie or something? It's been pretty lonely this last month. I've got a couple of days open next week while the subcontractors are busy doing their thing at the school."

Lucy picked up his money, dropped three bills on the floor, and unconsciously gave Matt a great view of her perky ass when she bent to pick them up.

He fought the urge to bend across the counter for a better inspection.

She straightened and took a deep breath, which caused her breasts to swell slightly.

Matt placed a hand over his heart and hoped his erection wouldn't pop back to attention. His tanned upper arm bunched.

"I promise I'm a safe guy to be with. Mavis can vouch for me that I used to be a Boy Scout."

He loved the sound of her soft laugh.

"I…" she shrugged. "I guess a movie would be fun."

"Okay! Say, do you have Saturday night off? We could go out to Angelo's for some Italian food first. I'm a diehard Italian cuisine buff. I'm tired of eating alone. I think it would be fun."

Lucy watched the straight line of his white teeth appear when he smiled. Her stomach went from a quiver to an all out jumping match. Matt was the most handsome guy she had ever encountered, and he wanted to take her on a date, to Angelo's no less. Her wish was coming true.

Chapter Two: The Proposition

Lucy carefully applied a thin base of lipstick, trying to contain her excitement at the coming evening. A quick glance at the clock on the bathroom wall told her that Matt would arrive within fifteen minutes.

Saturday hadn't come fast enough for Lucy. Matt had come into the café for lunch every day since Tuesday. He made small talk and burned her with his hot gaze as she waited tables. She did her best not to stare at him longingly when he wasn't looking. He had ignited a fire in her that had been out of fuel for far too long.

By the time the day of the planned movie arrived, Lucy's home had started to show the effects of her daydreaming about Matt. Three plates, six glasses, and a vase lay shattered in the dumpster at the end of the driveway. A burned frying pan joined the clutter only that morning. Lucy had started breakfast and ended up sitting on her porch to stare absently into the yard, thinking about what Matt's lips would taste like against hers. He would kiss her goodnight, wouldn't he? No man looked at a woman the way Matt ogled her if he didn't at least have some kissing in mind. The smoke detector was what shook her from her reverie and sent her racing back into the house.

As she straightened above the sink and adjusted a wayward red curl, her tabby cat jumped onto the vanity surface, rubbed himself against Lucy's hand, and purred contentedly when he received a scratch behind the ears.

"Good evening, Mr. Pibbs." A smile curved Lucy's lips when the cat purred louder. "You know, don't you, that you'll be spending the evening by yourself? I've managed to procure a date with a handsome man named Matt. He's the reason your dinner has been late over the last few days. Sorry about that. I've been a little distracted." Mr. Pibbs meowed when he recognized the word dinner. "He plans to take me to dinner—and of all places, Angelo's—and then to a movie. What do you think about that?"

The cat leapt from the ledge and skittered out the door on his way to the kitchen. Turning back to the mirror, Lucy shot one more glance at her curly auburn hair. "Hmmm—I'd give anything to be a blonde. I look like a sixteen-year-old girl with this shade." She grabbed her brush, ran it through her long unbound tresses one more time, and hurried after Mr. Pibbs to feed him his supper.

* * * * *

Lucy sat on her porch swing and watched Matt's black Suburban turn into the drive. Clenching her hands in her lap to stop the instant trembling, she stood, smiled, and waited for him at the top of the steps.

Matt waved when he got out of the vehicle, and Lucy's nervous smile widened. She observed his massive stature as he walked up the paved sidewalk and, from nowhere, an image of his naked body on top of hers flashed through her mind. She nearly toppled to the ground with the thought.

Approaching her, Matt's eyes narrowed. Up to now, he had only seen her in a white waitress uniform with comfortable shoes and a thick braid down her back. Now, deep red waves cascaded around satiny shoulders. The sight of Lucy dressed in a clinging emerald green sleeveless dress was far better than anything he could have imagined. His dark gaze swept the entire length of her body. Her arms and endlessly long legs were slightly tanned and sprinkled with light freckles, as was her face. Painted toenails peeked out from platform sandals. He knew without a double that his large hands would be able to span the nipped waistline above gently curved hips. But it was her breasts that got his heart to beat a little faster. They were generous in size with nipples that pressed hard against the soft material of her dress.

He stopped at the end of the sidewalk and wordlessly gazed up at her.

"Hello, Matt."

"Hi, Lucy." He nodded his head with a smile. "I've got to say, you look absolutely stunning tonight."

A slight flush reddened Lucy's cheeks. *It was worth every bloody cent I paid for this dress just to hear you say that.* She nervously smoothed the material over her hips with her hands.

The innocent motion rocked Matt to his core. He raised his arm and gently took her hand in his. "Should we go?"

* * * * *

"I feel bad that we missed the movie. Seeing a show was the reason you asked me out tonight." Lucy grinned and sipped at her expensive wine.

He observed her smile across the white tablecloth. The candle's glow sparkled in her emerald eyes. Beautiful red hair swirled around her bare upper arms. Matt's palm tightened around his wine goblet in an effort not to reach out and run his fingers through the satiny length. "I had totally forgotten that we were going to do that." Four pleasant hours had passed, and he hadn't even realized it. Leaning back in his chair, he was the picture of contentment. "Lucy, I can't tell you how much I enjoyed the conversation tonight."

"Me, too." She stared at him over the rim of her wineglass. "I hope I haven't bored you with all the details of my home remodel." She had latched onto the subject, knowing that he was in construction and it was something they could both relate to.

His quiet stare was slightly unnerving. "I want to say something, and I hope you won't take this the wrong way."

She remained calm even though her heart sank. *He's bored. This will be our last date...*

"I don't know what I expected tonight...well, yes I do. I figured I'd be sopping up spilled water out of my lap or picking you off the ground—especially when I saw those sexy shoes you're wearing."

"Matt—"

He held up his hand to stop anything she was about to say. "Don't be embarrassed. Even in this dim light, I can see that you're blushing. In fact—" he leaned forward and touched her cheek lightly with a steady finger, "—the color extends to here." His finger trailed a slow, sensuous path down across her chin, past her slender neck, and rested just above where her cleavage started.

Lucy wondered if anyone watched them. She didn't care. She also wondered if he could feel her heart pounding beneath his feathery touch as she fought to keep her breath steady. His penetrating observation was not what she had thought he was going to say.

"I'm going to be honest with you." His tongue moistened his lips. "I left my apartment tonight thinking about what it would feel like to have you beneath me—what it would feel like to hold your breasts in my hands."

Lucy swallowed—and quit breathing.

"Don't get me wrong. I still want your body." His hand trailed down to her arm where it lay on the table. He rubbed his thumb across her forearm until he held her trembling hand. "I just don't think I want a one-night stand. I haven't been with a woman for a while. I had more or less sworn off them. But you?" His head shook slowly. "You have captivated me, and I want to see where this thing that you've aroused in me will go. I have a proposition for you. I don't want to play the game of teenagers flirting across a room or pretending to accidentally brush against one another. I don't want to spend weeks getting to know you better. Sleep with me tonight. I'm a man and you're a beautiful woman. I want to be inside you and not wait another night longer to do it. I want your body wrapped around me."

Lucy nearly fainted. No man had ever been as honest with her as Matt was being right now. And hadn't she thought about lying beneath him, of having his lips pressed against hers? She hadn't gone any further with her fantasy because it was something she didn't think would ever happen. Not with a man like Matt and a clumsy girl like her.

She held out her wineglass, waiting for him to refill it. He complied silently, never taking his eyes from hers.

Lucy brought the goblet to her lips, tilted the glass, and drained the contents. Breathing deeply to clear her head, she tucked her purse beneath her arm and stood.

Matt watched her warily.

Lucy smiled down at him and touched his hair where it rested against his collar—it was something she had wanted to do all evening. "I believe we need to go back to my house and finish our date."

* * * * *

Once in Matt's vehicle, Lucy wasn't quite so sure she could be as brave as she portrayed. Sitting in the dark with only the dashboard lights to outline their profiles, she turned her head to stare at the man beside her.

What do I know about him? That he was someone from Mavis' past? He's got a brother because that's what she said. He never said anything else about his family. I'm the one who spilled her guts all night while he simply listened and smiled.

But he wants me! Within the hour, he'll have made love to me already. Did I shave my legs? Oh, yeah, I did. What about birth control? Okay, relax, Luce. You've stayed on the pill. I don't have any rubbers secreted away. Is he clean? Of course he is. Look at him! She turned her gaze to the window and stared out at the various homes with light shining behind their half-closed curtains. *I can't believe I'm sitting here, knowing that I'm going to be naked with him shortly…what the heck am I going to do? The last time I had sex was…?*

"Having second thoughts?"

Lucy jumped at the sound of his voice. But before she could say anything, he continued.

"I'm not a serial killer, Lucy. I'm an honest, disease-free man that is hot for you. I've watched you all week. You don't even realize how sexy you are."

"I'm not," she mumbled. She'd admit that out loud, but would keep to herself that she'd lost enough weight over the last four years and didn't consider herself the fat little girl anymore.

"The hell you're not! I've had half an erection all night just sitting at the same table as you."

"Oh, geez…" Lucy ran her hand through her hair. No one had ever been *this* honest with her.

Matt patted her bare thigh, and then placed both hands on the wheel. One more block and they would be at Lucy's house at the end of town. "Just say the word and we can put this night on hold. I don't want to wait to go to bed with you, but I also don't want you to do anything you're not ready for. When I hold a woman in my arms and make love to her, I want her complete attention and no misgivings come morning."

"I…Matt…it's just that I've never had anyone be as honest as you're being. I'm no virgin, but what if one of us discovers that they really didn't like being with the other? What happens then? Do we shake hands and say, "don't call me"? That would be pretty awkward, don't you think? Especially since you're going to be living here for another year."

Matt clicked on the blinker and pulled into Lucy's driveway. After putting the vehicle in park, he turned the engine off, swiveled in his seat, and stared at her. He leaned across the seat, pulled her body next to his, and whispered, "I'm going to kiss you. When I'm done, you tell me if you want me to go home or if you ask me in the morning how I like my eggs done."

Lucy's eyes fluttered shut just before their lips touched. Matt played gently around her closed mouth; tender, soft kisses were dropped across her cheek. Feeling the tense set of her shoulders, he whispered his lips across the soft spot below her ear. "Mmmm…you smell delicious…" He took her hand in his. "I want you to know what you're doing to me."

Lucy gasped softly when her hand was pressed against the huge bulge at his crotch. She gasped again and her mouth sagged open when he imprisoned her hand more firmly before he arched his covered erection against her palm.

Matt took advantage of her surprise and swirled his tongue inside her mouth. Suddenly, his hand left hers and traveled up her midriff to cup one of her breasts.

A deep purr sounded from Lucy's throat as she pressed his hand closer, her doubts fading into oblivion. "Oh, God, Matt."

His tongue delved deeper as he whipped up an even more heated response by massaging her other breast.

She was enslaved by his eagerness, totally forgetting that they were trying to decide if they would have sex tonight or not. Matt had set her blood on fire with just his gentle touches and his tongue in her mouth. She slid further into the seat, dragged her fingers from his erection, and grasped his hand more firmly around her breast. "Oh, that feels so good…it's been so long…"

"You feel good. I love how your breast fits inside my hand. Christ, you're one sexy woman." He managed to free his hand from her clutches and massage his way back down to her stomach. Lucy now met his tongue with her own thrusts. Small moans filled the darkness of the vehicle.

Matt dropped his hand further, found the hem of her dress, and slipped beneath it. Lucy groaned when his fingers whispered up the smooth expanse of an inner thigh.

"Spread your legs wider for me."

Lucy's knees parted slightly, allowing enough room for Matt to slip his hand more firmly between her legs. His fingers came in contact with her silk bikini briefs. He ran his hand over the heated softness, feeling the pubic hair curled beneath the thin material. He wasn't about to waste any time trying to get her panties off and searched for the elastic band that encased one leg. Gently, he slid his middle finger between the warm layer of skin and silk, working his way down until he felt the wet heat of her pussy.

Lucy bucked and Matt impaled her with his finger. She was tight and hotter than anything he had encountered in a long time. He withdrew his finger and flicked her swollen clit with her own moisture, and then dipped back inside her.

Lucy panted against his ear, groaning with the flame that began to burn her. Her hips undulated as her pussy grasped at his finger.

"I knew you'd be like this — eager and excited — like a little red-headed tigress..."

Matt worked another finger inside the stretched elastic of her panties and plunged inside her. Lucy met each thrust with her own driving force, not even worrying that she lay with her dress up around her hips, one foot pressed against the steering wheel for more leverage, and with almost a complete stranger half over her with his tongue down her throat. She was in heaven with the way he played her body. Her hips surged forward.

The orgasm slammed through her. Lucy's hand flailed wildly, and then cupped his hand with hers to hold it tightly against her pubic bone as she rolled with the waves of heat. The press of Matt's hot lips against her breasts through the material of her dress and his thick fingers inside her drove her wild. There was no embarrassment, only this hot, satisfied relief that his presence had brought her to.

Matt withdrew his fingers, slid one of them up and down between her slick folds, and relished the quick catch of breath in her throat and the way she jumped beneath his hand when he circled her clit once more.

"You're pussy is still hot. I want to fuck you, Lucy, but I don't want to do it here. Let me come inside and spend the night. This is only a touch of how your body reacted to me. I want you."

Lucy untangled her foot from the steering wheel and dropped it weakly to the seat. Her heavy lids finally opened.

Matt stared at her swollen lips that were so close to his own, and then smiled when her stunned gaze met his.

"Oh, Matt."

He imagined her stretching lazily like a cat with just those two words.

She smiled wider. "I bet you like your eggs scrambled."

Chapter Three: A Bit of Heaven

He helped her to sit upright, kissed her lightly, and popped his door open. In a flash, he rounded the front of the vehicle and lifted Lucy from the seat. She wrapped her legs around his waist and kissed him as he hurried up the sidewalk and onto the porch.

"The key is under the mat." Lucy giggled hysterically as soon as the words left her mouth.

"What?" He set her down and bent to retrieve the key.

"The mat...you know, like *Matt*." She giggled again and straightened the dress around her hips.

He smiled up. "I didn't think you had that much to drink."

Lucy yanked him to a standing position and wrapped her arms around his neck. "I'm drunk with you. You've made me hot all week by just watching me at the restaurant. I can't believe we're here. I can't believe what you do to me." She stood on her tiptoes and nuzzled his lips. "Thank you for back there. That was some of the best sex I've had in a long time."

Matt pulled her close with one arm as he inserted the key into the lock and opened the door. "That's nothing, honey. That was just a little foreplay compared to what it's going to be like in about five minutes. I've got a hard-on stiffer than a board, and I plan to get rid of it."

He pulled her into the living room and slammed the door behind him. A second later, he dropped his mouth and captured hers in yet another kiss that stole her breath. Breaking away, Matt cupped her face with his large hands, ran his tongue across the seam of her mouth, and sighed deeply. "I don't know what it is about you, but you make me hotter than any woman I've ever known."

Lucy's head nodded in response. "You do the same to me. I've never become so..." she searched for the word, "...so enraptured with a man so quickly. I want you to know that I don't normally jump into bed with someone so fast. In fact, it's been almost two years since I've been with anyone. The last guy stole my heart, then threw it on the ground and stomped on it. I'm not declaring anything here, but I hope this can continue. I don't want a one-night stand either."

As she spoke, Matt reached up to caress her breasts, and then wrapped his arms around her slim waist. Lucy's head fell back as he licked the spot below her ear.

"Oh, Matt. What is this—why do you turn me on like you do?"

"I don't know, Luce. I just know that I want to be inside you." He bent, placed one arm below her ass, and hauled her body up and into his embrace. "Where's your bedroom?"

Lucy caressed his firm jaw with the tips of her fingers and stared into the smoldering eyes above her. "Up the stairs. First door on the right."

Matt took the steps two at a time. He used his body to open the door and stepped into her bedroom. For some reason, it didn't look like he expected it to. A canopy capped the bed with frilly white lace hanging from the rungs. An antique vanity with an ornate oval mirror stood against one wall. Small baskets filled with yarn, an old rocking chair, and shelves filled with books finished out the decor. The room was cozy, welcoming, and more organized than he thought it would be. It was easy to see that Lucy had created a small haven for herself. His eyes shifted back to the mirror. He crossed the room, stood before the vanity, and let Lucy's body slowly glide the length of his as he steadied her on her feet.

Pulling her close to his chest, he watched their reflection in the mirror as he ran his hands down her back and cupped her ass. The curved globes were soft, yet firm beneath the silky material. God, he wanted her, and he wanted this first time to be something memorable for both of them. Suddenly, an idea hit him.

Matt straightened, shoved the stool that was placed before the vanity out of the way with his foot, and turned Lucy so she could see herself. "I want you to watch what I do to you."

Lucy's mouth opened with a slight gasp, immediately caught up in his sensual suggestion.

"I want to make love to you here for the first time." He nuzzled her neck, but watched her eyes closely in the shimmering pane, and then reached out and clicked on the small lamp that hung on the wall above the mirror. "Do you have any objections?"

Lucy's stomach flipped. Matt had cast a spell over her. She craved his hands on her; she longed to have his penis sliding inside her. Reaching for his hands at her waist, she placed them over her swollen breasts, and rested the back of her head against his chest, never taking her gaze from his in the mirror.

Matt ran his tongue across the exposed area of her collarbone. He squeezed her breasts together, then ran a light path down her stomach to the apex of her legs where he kneaded her mound through the material. "I know what this feels like. Your pussy is hot and wet and tight." His groan matched hers. "Oh, God, so tight."

His fingers left her to travel to the zipper at her back.

A feeling of loss skittered through Lucy's body when her heated massage ended until she realized that he was about to undress her. She had never experienced anything so simply sensual as watching a man disrobe her, knowing what the end result was going to be. The anticipation clogged her throat.

The sound of the zipper opening echoed in the room. The only other noise was Matt's slightly heavier breathing in her ear. She watched his hands slide beneath the material covering her cleavage. Slowly, the spaghetti straps were removed from her shoulders and pulled down over her arms until her lacy strapless bra was exposed.

Matt stepped back and slid the bunched dress over her slim hips. A second later, Lucy stepped from the center of material at her feet. She stood clad in only the bra and a lacy pair of matching bikini underwear. The sensation of watching her breasts expand slightly as she concentrated on even breaths was mesmerizing. She was never so hot to have a man inside her as she was at this moment.

He rested his palms on her hips, nuzzled her neck again, and stared at her in the mirror. "You've got a beautiful body. I can't wait to fuck you."

"Matt, please...I don't know how much more of this I can take."

"Anticipation, Lucy, anticipation. This is half the fun." One hand snaked up to a covered breast as the other slid back to her crotch. His thumb played about the elastic waist, burning a path across the smooth skin of her belly. For the second time that night, his fingers slipped inside her underwear. "Your pubic hair is soft, but I've felt your pussy lips. I know they're softer."

Her eyelids lowered as her mouth sagged opened again. Matt's body kept her from wilting to the floor.

"Open your eyes, Lucy. I don't want you to miss anything."

She obeyed as little pants left her lips. "I feel like I'm going to come again. That's never happened before — not this fast."

"You're going to come all night," he whispered beside her ear. "Do you want to have orgasms all night?"

"Oh, God...yes...yes!"

Matt trailed a finger into her wet slit, flicked her clitoris, and enjoyed how her entire body jumped at the contact. He teased her for a second, and then withdrew his hand from her panties.

To keep her knees from buckling, Lucy's fingers grasped his arm that had found its way around her midriff.

Matt easily freed the clasp between her breasts with his free hand and tossed her bra to the dresser. His eyes narrowed as he watched himself touch her erect nipples for the first time. He rolled the tips between his fingers, then covered them both with his hands, squeezing lightly and wanting to have them in his mouth. "Raise your arm, Lucy. I want to suck on your nipple, but I want you to see it."

She did so and watched him move in the reflection until he sat on one side of the vanity's surface.

"Don't look at me. Just watch the mirror." Matt leaned forward and captured a nipple in his mouth.

Lucy was spellbound, watching the back of his dark head blot out a portion of her white breast and feeling the suction of his lips as they tugged at her nipple. It was an erotic experience to separate the two senses and discover so much enjoyment.

As Matt teased her nipple with his tongue, she continued to gaze into the mirror. His hand slid over the flatness of her belly and into the front of her bikini briefs. Once again, the separation of senses constricted her stomach muscles. Lucy's arm dropped to run her fingers through the thick dark waves of his hair.

Matt cupped his hand and pressed his palm against her, applying pressure to her clitoris, gently grinding against her. Lucy widened her stance to allow him access, but he didn't enter her with his finger.

"Matt..."

He withdrew his hand from her panties and his lips from her nipple, stood, and moved behind her again. Lucy made to turn toward him, but he halted her, forcing her to continue to look into the mirror. Hooking his thumbs at the elastic of her bikini waistband, Matt tugged her underwear over her hips and down to her ankles. Lucy tossed the flimsy bit of lace to the side with her foot.

Stepping back, he pulled his polo shirt over his head as he locked gazes with her in the mirror. A quick flip of his belt had the leather strap open and his zipper came down next. He dropped his pants and kicked them away.

Lucy stared at the huge bulge beneath his briefs, licked her lips, and waited for him to free his penis.

"You make me hard, Lucy." Matt dragged his underwear down his long, muscular legs and his briefs joined his pants a few feet away. His cock was thick and long, throbbing in her direction.

She knew it would look like this—she had anticipated the sight of it since he'd placed her hand over his cock in the truck. "I want to turn around, Matt."

His head shook, accompanied by a sly grin. "Oh, no, Lucy. I'll come to you." He stepped slightly in front of her, took her hand, and wrapped her fingers around his cock. She watched their reflection as he pulled her hand up and down his length. "I'm going to put this in you, and then you're going to watch yourself come in the mirror."

She was slightly confused. "How?"

He moved back behind her. "I'll show you," he whispered close again. "Trust me."

"I do."

Matt's hand moved down over her buttocks and between her legs. "Spread your legs a little more. Hang onto my arm if you need to."

Lucy grabbed the arm at her waist and spread her stance. She watched Matt's hand appear between her legs to caress her pubic mound from behind. Suddenly, his middle finger disappeared as she felt it reach up inside her. Hot shards of excitement pierced her belly as she ground against his hand, and then suddenly, his thick finger was gone.

Matt grabbed the stool and pulled it behind him, dropped to the surface, and pulled her back against him. "Rest your ass on my lap. Put your feet up on the vanity and spread your legs." Lucy hurried to do what he asked; her clitoris throbbed with the need to find release.

She had never seen herself spread before a mirror. Her slit glistened in the lamplight; moisture dampened the curly red pubic hair. Feeling Matt's hand wiggle under her ass, she lifted slightly until his hand came into view between her legs again.

"Watch what I'm going to do to you."

She stared unblinkingly as a long finger disappeared into her vagina, only to slide back out, dart in a circular motion around her clitoris, and then disappear again. Matt began to pump with a steady rhythm.

The muscles in Lucy's entire body constricted as the hot pleasure built, but she continued to stare at his hand that gave her so much pleasure. Another finger joined the one inside her as Matt dropped his other hand to roll her clitoris from the front. Lucy ground against him with an unladylike grunt.

"Come for me again, Lucy." His fingers darted in and out of her pussy.

Lucy gasped and squeezed her body around his thrusting digits.

Matt's pressure against her clitoris increased with the speed of his tortuous but wonderful assault.

"Matt!"

Matt panted against her ear as he did his best to hold her undulating body from sliding off his lap.

Lucy's body jerked in tight little thrusts as her breasts burned with heat, but she never took her eyes from her crotch. Finally, the waves subsided and her feet dropped limply to the floor as Matt's fingers left her pussy to find their way to her heaving breasts. She heard the chuckle in his words when he spoke.

"Twice you've come now, and I haven't even put my cock in you."

Her head lolled against his chest.

"Did you enjoy that?"

"Matt...no one has ever done that to me. It was sexy and erotic and...I'll never be able to come again tonight. I've reached my peak."

Another throaty chuckle sounded against the softness of her earlobe. "Oh, my dear, Lucy. Never under estimate a diamond in the rough." He stood, perched her on the stool to face him, and spread her knees. "Lean back and put your elbows on the vanity to support yourself. I'm going to make a liar out of you."

Matt dropped to his knees, reached out, and stroked the outside of her pussy. With a sly smile, he spread her thighs wider, bent forward and licked her clitoris. "You taste like sex should. If I would've known what you had under that waitress uniform, I would have found my way here sooner."

Lucy hardly heard him. She was so overcome by the instant heat that started to spread again that her hand moved with a will of its own and rested on the back of his head, urging him on to more delights.

Matt slipped a finger into her, turned his hand, and stroked the upper side of her vagina. His tongue danced between her wet folds.

"Oh...Matt...I..."

He captured her clitoris and rolled his tongue around the swollen bud. Lucy wiggled on the bench, her body joining the dance he had started. Matt sucked endlessly, working her like a fine instrument.

Suddenly he stood, dragged her from the stool, and bent her forward until she realized what he wanted her to do. Lucy braced her hands on the surface of the vanity and spread her legs. Matt hurried behind her and entered her pussy with a savage stroke.

Lucy didn't need to be told to watch their reflection. Her heavy lidded gaze met his hot one as she worked herself up and down the length of his long cock. Matt slammed into her time after time. Her breasts swung crazily, her fingers turned white where they gripped the edge of the dresser, and she smiled back at him. His face changed. Matt grit his teeth and met her challenge.

A massive orgasm exploded inside her as Matt's rhythm changed to short, hard strokes. When he shoved his cock inward with one last savage thrust and gripped her hips tightly, she realized he was coming. Lucy squeezed the muscles of her vagina and shook around his pulsing erection.

Perspiration beaded both their foreheads when Matt withdrew, lifted her into his arms, and crossed to the bed. Both gasped heavily for air as they lay beside each other, waiting for their strength to return. Before it happened, they fell into a deep sleep across the top of the frilly bedspread.

Chapter Four: Getting to Know You

Lucy's body floated, bobbing gently with the rhythm of the waves. The rays of the hot sun heated her blood. Warm water enveloped her body as ripples brushed across the tips of her breasts. She dreamed. She dreamed of a man named Matt—a man who had come into her life one day and changed her world.

A smile flitted across her lips. The water rose to her chin. Lucy was safe and secure in the warm caressing liquid that now entered her body. In fact, the heat filled her vagina, urging her to join the dipping of the tide as it moved in and out of her slowly, taking her upwards toward the blue sky, and then back down to rest in the bottom of the swell.

"Lucy…" her name whispered past her ear. "Come with me…"

Her thick lashes batted momentarily as she forced herself awake. "Matt?"

He slid his cock into her pussy again and smiled down at the sleepy look on her face. He tipped his head and swirled his tongue into her open mouth and back out. "I couldn't wait for you to wake up, so…"

Lucy lifted her knees and wrapped her calves over his clenching buttocks, imprisoning him inside her. "Wonderful—" she whispered breathlessly, "—what a beautiful way to wake up."

Matt increased his tempo slightly. "I've been lying here waiting for you to wake up. Your naked body was too much for me to resist."

"I was dreaming about a hot sun and warm water filling me, but it was you all along." She arched against him, urging him on to an even greater tempo. "Fill me, Matt."

He leaned on an elbow, grasped her leg and dragged her knee over his shoulder, and stroked harder.

Lucy hissed with instant satisfaction the new position brought. Every stroke Matt took, he found the opportunity to grind against her clitoris, finding pleasure in the small moans springing from the back of her throat.

Matt began to pound into her, and Lucy met him stroke for stroke, her tight body wrapped around him, refusing to let him escape completely. Suddenly, each thrust became one long glorious slide; separated from the next by the fact that Lucy nearly left the bed's surface each time he rammed her cervix.

"That's it! Oh, Matt, I'm…"

Her pussy quivered around his hard length when he buried himself inside her.

"Lucy!" his head lolled against the crook of her neck. "I can't get enough of you." He stroked three times to finish emptying himself, helped her to disentangle her leg from his shoulder, and rolled to his back, bringing her body with him.

Lucy lay across his torso, her breasts crushed against the wiry hair on his chest, and stared down at him with breathless pants. She bent her head and drew a kiss from his lips. "You are the most amazing man I know."

He gave her a peck on the nose. "I beg to differ. You are something. I watched you while you slept. More than once you sighed deeply, and I don't think I've ever seen anyone as contented as you were."

"And why wouldn't I be? I've had some of the best sex ever in the last—" She glanced at her wind-up clock. It was six-thirty in the morning. "—ten hours. I don't have to work today, and the wonderful man who made me come time after time is still in my bed. Who wouldn't be contented?"

Matt reached up and tucked the curtain of her hair behind one ear. His finger wrapped itself within a wayward curl, giving him leverage to pull her mouth to his. When he was through kissing Lucy, a grin curved his moist lips. "As much as I'd like to lay here all morning and play, you did intimate last night that you would cook me breakfast. How about I help you, then we'll clean up and think of something to do today."

"I can think of something to do," she giggled.

Instantly, he knew what she hinted at. Matt squeezed her round butt in response. "You can bet your sweet little ass that we'll be having a lot more of each other today. That's a promise! But, for now? I'm really hungry!"

Lucy kissed him one more time and rolled from his body. Matt watched her stroll across the room, enjoying the sight of her round bare ass and long, shapely legs before she tossed on a robe. It amazed him that she moved like a sleek feline when naked, but fumbled her way through the café when she was in uniform, breaking dishes and spilling water. He shook his head in wonder and quickly joined her to head downstairs.

✻ ✻ ✻ ✻ ✻

Lucy pushed the remains of her breakfast around the center of her plate. She could care less about eating. Matt had awakened something in her that had long lain dormant. In fact, she didn't remember feeling this way at all with her last boyfriend—even after having been with him for an extended period of time.

She glanced up to watch him rinse off his plate at the sink; Matt standing in her kitchen in his briefs seemed natural as hell; like they had been together for a long time. She had herself a new boyfriend. *Is that what he is? Is he my boyfriend now or just a simple sex partner for the moment?* She didn't want it to be just *simple.* Lucy had fallen in love sometime during the erotic ritual before the mirror and the beautiful awakening this morning and there wasn't a damn thing she could do about it.

Play it safe. That's what I'll do. Hell, I can't do that. He might get bored. Watching him move about the kitchen as if he'd been doing it all his life, Lucy sighed quietly. Even Mr. Pibbs had fallen in love, and he didn't extend himself to just anyone. Right now, the damned cat rubbed against Matt's bare ankles, waiting to be picked up and scratched behind the ear.

"Do you have cat food somewhere? I think he's hungry."

"Hmmmm?"

"Cat food, Luce. Where is it?"

"There's a can opened already in the fridge."

Matt opened the door to the refrigerator and had Mr. Pibbs' bowl filled in a flash. Lucy shook her head as he cooed and told the cat what a good boy he was. This sure didn't seem like the man who had turned her inside out over the course of one night.

"Mr. Pibbs seems taken with you."

Matt smiled as he ambled back to the table. "I used to have a cat. Used to take a lot of ribbing because of it, too. When my family left Colby and moved to another city, I found this beat-up tomcat living under the steps of our new home. I got him some milk and a couple of hot dogs because I felt sorry for him. That cat followed me everywhere I went until the day he died." His eyes were now on Mr. Pibbs, who lapped greedily at his food.

"You know, Matt, that's the first personal thing you've said to me. I've spilled my guts about renovating this house, about not having any family, about my job. Yet, you haven't said one word."

Matt simply shrugged his nonchalance. "Not much to tell."

"Are you trying to hide something from me?" Lucy watched him closely.

Matt's head fell back as a chuckle left his throat.

Lucy loved the way his unshaven jaw looked in the morning light.

"Okay, Lucy. I'm not some secret spy or a fugitive on the run. Go ahead, shoot. Ask me anything you want."

She crossed her arms beneath her robed breasts and smiled at his obvious attempt to put her at ease. "Okay. Do you have any family?"

"Doesn't everyone at some time or other?"

"Don't be a smart ass."

He just smiled again. "Let's see. I have a mother and father that live in a retirement community in Florida."

"Any siblings?"

"Yup. One brother."

"Older or younger?"

"Older."

"Does he live around here?"

"Why? Planning to try him out and see which one of us is the best Diamond?"

Lucy rolled her eyes heavenward.

"All right. He lives about a half a day's drive from here. We work together when I'm not based in a hotel somewhere. Nice guy."

"What's his name?"

"Jake—or Jacob if you want to be formal about it."

"Hmm. Matt and Jake—Matthew and Jacob. You're mother must have thought the two of you were saints."

Matt threw back his head and laughed loudly. "Well, I can guarantee you, I'd never want to have kids someday that were like the two of us when we were younger!"

Lucy leaned forward, placed her elbows on the table, and rested her chin in the palm of one hand. "Well, you just answered my next question. What are you, thirty-something?"

"I'll be thirty-one in September. By the way—how old are you?"

"What do you think?"

"No way, Luce. I'm not going to fall into that trap."

"I'm twenty-seven. Back to the subject. How come at the ripe old age of thirty, you don't' have a wife and kids? Let's be serious here. You're one handsome guy. You seem to have your head pretty well squared on your shoulders. You must be doing well. You drive an expensive vehicle and were pretty nicely dressed when you picked me up last night. Even though I like you in your present attire."

Matt contemplated the woman who sat across from him. The fleeting thought lit in his brain that if he had met Lucy years ago, he might not be running from a rotten relationship now. He mentally shook away an image of a blonde woman pleading with him for attention. "I was in a relationship with a woman for the last four years. Never married her — didn't want to spend the rest of my life with someone who was so needy. Hence the reason I opted to work on this job. I needed space — and a place where she didn't know where I was. What about you? You're one sexy lady to be all alone."

"I wasn't up until three years ago when I moved here. I was with a guy I met after graduation. He promised me the moon, but broke my heart when he found someone who had a lot more class than me. He wasn't very nice when he told me his parents didn't approve of a girl who looked like she had just walked off the farm."

"Their loss,"

Lucy shrugged. "It took a long time to realize that I was better off without such snobs in my life." She mechanically piled her glass and fork on her plate, rose from the table, and walked to the sink, thinking about their earlier conversation. "Is this woman out of your life just temporarily, or do you think it's completely over?"

"It's done. I haven't spoken with her for three months." He swiveled on his chair and watched her load the dishwasher. "I told you last night that I wasn't up for a one-night stand. I'll admit that the idea of having a little sex was the only thing on my mind when I first asked you out. I'm an honest guy, Lucy. I don't feel that way anymore. I want to keep seeing you — and not just for the great sex. You intrigue me. You've got this soft, innocent side with your freckled nose and blushing cheeks. Yet...you've got one helluva sexy body that blows me away."

Be brave, Lucy. She shut the door on the dishwasher, crossed to him, and ran her fingers across his whiskered jaw. "I feel the same way, Matt. I've thought about nothing but you since the day we met. It just feels so natural to have you here in my kitchen. But what about this other woman? Someday she'll find you again." Lucy did her best to keep her features relaxed, but the thought of having to contend with a woman from his past scared the hell out of her.

Matt easily saw her struggle. He captured her hand and kissed her palm as he smiled up at her. Lucy bent forward and touched her lips to his. As the kiss deepened, he found her other hand, pulled it down, and rested it on his covered penis. His cock immediately hardened beneath her light touch. "And it seems natural to do this. You've done something to me, and I don't know if I'll ever have enough of you. I'm done with that other woman. I have been for some time now."

Matt's breath caught in his throat when her hand slid inside his underwear. A second later, his eyebrows rose in surprise when she straightened, opened her robe, and slid it off her shoulders. She stood totally at ease with her milky white breasts and creamy skin on display, a calculating gleam in her green gaze.

Reaching for his hand, Lucy placed it between her legs. "Put your finger in me."

Matt was amazed. One minute, she was like a hesitant teenager, waiting to see if he would reject her. The next, she was a naked wanton, promising him pleasure with just the look in her eyes. He stroked the outside of her pussy, then dipped a finger inside, wondering what she had planned next.

Lucy's head lolled back for a second as she let him play, making her ready for easy entry.

Matt rolled her clit with his thumb, wanting to suck her nipples, but deciding that this was Lucy's game. He would let her lead wherever she wanted to go.

Her chin came forward as her hand dropped to his erection once more. Yanking gently on his waistband, she was able to free his penis for her inspection. "I see you're ready for me again."

Matt remained silent as his finger slipped from her wet heat.

Lucy slowly straddled his lap. Bending at the knees, she grasped his penis and rubbed the head up and down her wet slit. A smile appeared on her lips when a whoosh of air left Matt's lungs.

Placing the head of his cock near her opening, her smile widened when she slid the entire length of his rock hard erection. Matt circled her small waist with his hands and lay inside her, throbbing.

Lucy began to move up and down, sliding a hot path that drove the man on the chair to distraction.

Matt tilted his head and nipped at the smooth skin of one breast before catching an erect nipple between his teeth.

Lucy wiggled, finding it hard to maintain the momentum she had set. Her arms goosebumped. She tossed him a dare. "Is that all you've got? I want you to make me come."

He bit her nipple harder and heard her delighted gasp. She rode him as he thrust forward each time she slammed down on his cock. Matt encircled her with a powerful embrace, crushing her breasts to his chest, relishing the feel of her nipples as they whisked through the hair on his chest. The heat between the two lovers crackled.

One strong hand rested on the back of her head now while he guided his middle finger of the other into her mouth, letting her suck on it, imagining her tongue swirling around the head of his penis instead of his finger. That would come later.

Withdrawing his finger, he dropped his hand down to her ass that was spread open across his lap, followed her crack until he found her soft anus, and gently worked his moistened finger into her rectum. Lucy groaned with absolute pleasure against his lips and exploded with an orgasm a second later. Matt could feel the pulsing not only around his erection but also his finger, which spurred him on to his own release. He tucked his finger even deeper into her ass, using the strength of his palm resting against her ass to keep her impaled on his cock, and let his semen fill her.

Lucy fell forward and rested her head on his damp shoulder. Even though she was exhausted, she let him continue to finger her rectum, never having experienced the feeling before.

"Do you like this?" Matt breathed beside her ear. "Do you like sex this way?" His finger continued to tease her.

"No one has ever done this to me," she whispered back, ready to go again with the excitement that started to build once more.

"Do you want me to put my cock in your ass?" He sucked on her earlobe, amazed that he was getting an erection already with just the thought.

"I want you to...I want to see what it feels like."

He withdrew his finger, stood with her in his arms, and headed for the bedroom upstairs. Once he was there, he gently laid her on the bed. "Do you have anything like KY?"

Her eyes were glued to his hard penis. She shook her head slowly. "I've never had a need for something like that." Suddenly, her eyes lit up. "Wait a minute. Yes I do. There's a small tube in the back of the medicine cabinet. It was in a packet I got from the clinic once."

"Well, then, you roll onto your stomach, and I'll be right back."

Lucy stared at the bottom of the bed's canopy and didn't flip to her belly until she heard the medicine cabinet close. She waited breathlessly. She had read about anal sex, but never experienced it. If it was anything like what had happened in the kitchen, she was sure to enjoy Matt inside her.

He returned to the bedroom and approached the edge of the bed with a towel in his hand. Lucy glanced over her shoulder, her gaze hot with building desire. "I'm thinking that this will be more fun if you get me ready for you. Why don't you sit on the edge for a minute." Lucy scrambled up and scooted her ass across the bedspread. Matt handed her the tube. "Why don't you make sure I'm good and hard for you."

Squirting the jelly into her hand, Lucy reached for him, and spread the gel over his cock while stroking him from the base of his shaft to the tip of his penis. Just the action and the thought of where he was going to put it made her wet.

Matt closed his eyes and enjoyed the sensation of being held in her hand. Lucy never ceased to amaze him. He let the foreplay continue for a few minutes before he grasped her wrist and stared down. Bending forward, he kissed her waiting mouth and used the towel to wipe the excess gel from her palm. "I'm ready for you."

Wordlessly, she rolled to her stomach again. Matt grasped her waist and hauled her to the edge, positioning her knees so her ass was slightly raised. She lay there, spread and waiting for him. Rubbing a finger across his cock to moisten it, he used two fingers of his other hand to play with her pussy, dipping them in and out of her, surprised how eagerly she followed the motion.

"Christ, you're wet. You're ready for this, aren't you?"

"I want you in me, Matt. I want to do this."

He ran his gelled finger across her ass, hesitated at the opening of her rectum, then slowly worked into her. Lucy's hands grasped the bedspread. "Does that hurt you when I'm in that far?"

She clenched her teeth and shook her head.

Matt moved closer, took his cock in his hand and rested it against her. He simply hoped he wouldn't come too soon. Hot with anticipation, he slid slowly into her waiting rectum, his breaths coming in tiny pants of extreme pleasure. She was tight around him. He waited for her to move, to let him know it was tolerable to keep going.

Lucy rose up on her hands; her breathing matched his. "Oh, God..." She began to rock slowly against him. "Matt! Don't stop!"

Her urging was all he needed. He slid in further as she gasped in pleasure. Red hair cascaded wildly across her shoulders and down her back.

Matt's heart pounded. Lucy was completely and unabashedly at his disposal and loving every minute of it! She didn't want him to stop. Her reaction pierced his belly with heat, and he stroked harder.

A flash of another woman in the same position, begging him to stop, telling him she hated him, raced through his brain, but he flung it away. He was with Lucy; he was with a woman that urged him on; he was with someone he could spend the rest of his life with if he chose to.

Grasping her undulating hips tightly, Matt felt the waves of her orgasm as he came in spurts that sent heat racing through his groin.

Chapter Five: Love Grows

Lucy opened the door of the stainless steel refrigerator and set a stack of dirty plates on the rack beside a row of covered bowls that contained luncheon salads already prepared for the day's business. An entire month had passed since Matt had walked through the front doors and changed her life and they had been together every moment possible over the warm days of June.

She was drunk with passion and the fire he created when he touched her body. It had happened so fast that now she couldn't remember a time when he wasn't a part of her life. She tripped through her days with a smile plastered across her face—even when Pete berated her for her continual errors at the café. Nothing bothered her because she had found the man of her dreams. She was in love and that was all that mattered.

Letting the refrigerator door swing shut, Lucy leaned against the cool exterior with closed eyes. Just thinking of lying beside Matt the evening before caused a shiver to run down her spine.

"What the hell are you doing?"

Lucy's eyes snapped open. "What?"

Mavis gently rapped her knuckles on the top of Lucy's head. "Hello in there! I asked you what the hell you're doing? Lucy girl, you just put dirty plates in the refrigerator instead of the dishwasher!"

The younger woman stared at her as if Mavis had lost her mind. "What do you mean?"

Mavis gently grasped Lucy's shoulders and moved her out of the way. She proceeded to open the stainless door and jab a thumb at the dirty plates stacked inside. "This is what I mean."

She leaned closer and spied the red flush on her coworker's cheeks. "What the hell is that man doing to you? You make more mistakes around here than a teenage girl. I can't keep covering for you."

Lucy clasped her hands before her. "Sorry. I'm sorry, Mavis. I'm just having a hard time concentrating." She peeked up from beneath thick lashes and her full mouth broke into a huge grin. "Mavis! He's so wonderful! How did I ever get so lucky?"

The older woman closed the door of the fridge, crossed her arms over ponderous breasts, and leaned a thick shoulder against the stainless steel door. "So, you think this is the one?"

Lucy spun in a circle. "I know he's the one!" She grabbed Mavis' hand and dragged her to sit on two stools placed by the back door.

"Hey! It's not break time!" Pete tossed them an owly look from where he stood before the griddle.

"Kiss my ass, old man. Give us a little privacy before it gets busy in here. I'll take my break any goddamned time I please." Mavis was rewarded with another look of disgust before Pete stomped down the hall and into the employee bathroom. She glanced back at Lucy with a raised bushy eyebrow. "So, Matt has you in the palm of his hand? Oh, to be lucky enough to have a hunk like him chasing me!"

Lucy clasped the woman's hands and squeezed them with excitement. "Oh, Mavis. I've never been this happy."

"Well, that's easy to see! Have the two of you talked about the future at all?" She watched a flash of doubt race through the green eyes across from her. It was gone as quickly as it appeared. "Lucy, has Matt told you he loved you? Or is this thing between you purely physical?"

"He...he hasn't said it in so many words, but I know he will."

"Have you told him how you feel?"

The redhead simply shrugged her shoulders.

"You haven't, have you? What's holding you back?" She tipped her head and stared. "You do love him, don't you?"

"Of course I do. He treats me like a lady, buys me gifts, and turns my blood to fire."

"Sounds like how Frank acts. That doesn't mean he loves me or plans to marry me. Listen. Me and Frank are old and set in our ways. We like screwing each other because there's no commitment. It's just a great time and a way to get our urges out." She sat back. "What? Don't look so surprised. Old, fat people like to have sex, too." She shook her head. "But you and Matt are young. You have your whole life in front of you. I don't even have to ask if he's great in the sack—you can tell that by one glance at him and the look of total satisfaction on your face. Didn't you say once you wanted more than that? Wasn't your wish to find a man to take care of you and give you babies?"

"I don't want to push him. He'll tell me in his own good time."

* * * * *

Matt found it impossible to concentrate during the long days at the construction site. The picture of Lucy's naked body stretched wide across the bed had him in a constant state of having to hide his arousal.

He walked across the school's playground to the trailer that doubled as a makeshift construction office, relishing the cool air-conditioned space once he closed the door behind him, and plopped down into an old leather chair placed before a metal desk strewn with blueprints. It wasn't long before his feet rested on the surface with ankles crossed and his large hands clasped behind his head.

Lucy. The vision of her naked body morphed into a picture of her lovingly tending her garden beds. She glanced up with a beautiful smile to greet him and smoldering green eyes that were nearly hidden by the floppy brim of her white hat. Her nipples instantly hardened beneath the tight t-shirt that covered her bare breasts in the late June heat. Tanned legs unfolded as she leapt up from where she kneeled beside the flowerbed, revealing firm slender thighs—the same thighs she wrapped around his waist when he was pounding into her body.

"Christ almighty—" Warm air whistled out of his lungs when he dropped his feet to the floor and heaved himself from the chair. Staring out the dirty window, Matt didn't see the machinery that hauled away bits and pieces of the building the company was renovating. Instead, he saw Lucy's sheepish smile when she dropped an entire plate of turkey because she was rushing to feed him his dinner.

Matt snorted and shook his head. He wondered how she managed to get through the days without hurting herself with her constant fumbling and bumbling. "Shit!! I'm the one who takes the biggest brunt of it," he mumbled to the empty room and thought back to three nights earlier when he and Lucy were having a particularly rousing sex session. Lucy had pushed him backwards on the bed, made to straddle his erection, but accidentally kneed him in the balls. Matt's eyes nearly watered now with just the thought of instant agony that had stopped the sex between the two of them for the rest of the evening. Lucy had apologized and played with his penis for an hour to no avail. It was impossible to work up an erection after getting slammed like that. Instead, they ended up in a cuddle beneath the sheets and watched TV, simply enjoying each other's presence under the frilly canopy.

It hit him that very moment as he stared out the window, how much he had enjoyed that night, just holding her and loving her quiet presence. Being with Lucy was more than just the spine-tingling sex they shared. She warmed his heart with just her smile—he loved the quirky ways she accomplished things and her way of always being positive and stating she liked to keep her glass half-full—she was something. Matt sighed. He loved her.

He ran a hand through his wavy dark hair, stunned by the realization. He couldn't imagine never having her in his life. "Son of a bitch. Matt, you just fell for a woman. She stole your heart from right under your nose and you didn't know it until this moment."

He grabbed a bottle of water from the small fridge in the corner, chugged down three-quarters of it, and left the trailer with a much lighter step. Lucy was in for the night of her life.

* * * * *

Lucy leaned across the table with a lit match and waited until a small flame sputtered to life before moving to the matching candlestick on the other side of the centerpiece. They were eating at her home tonight instead of patronizing one of the local restaurants, and she wanted to make the evening special. It hit her, an awareness that made her giggle out loud, that she and Matt had never had sex on the dining room table. They had managed to make love just about every other place in the house, but for some reason, had bypassed the perfect surface she leaned across.

"Ouch!" Lucy flung the match that burned her fingertip and tried to shake the pain away by waving her hand. Her eyes frantically searched for the match that now lay extinguished on a clean plate. Thank goodness it hadn't burned the tablecloth.

"You're going to burn the house down one of these nights."

Lucy whirled around when she heard his voice coming from the other side of the screen door. "Matt! You're early."

The door slammed behind him as he held out his arms and waited for her welcoming hug. Lucy didn't disappoint him. She raced across the linoleum floor and wrapped her arms around his neck. The scent of his cologne had her brain instantly reeling with thoughts of the coming night.

"Ooo—you smell good! I missed you today."

He kissed the end of her nose. "You tell me that every day."

"Because it's true."

Matt sniffed the air over her shoulder when she hugged him again. "What's that delicious smell?"

"Pork roast, potatoes and carrots, and there's a cherry cheesecake—your favorite—in the fridge."

"How long before we eat?"

"At least another hour."

Slinging his arm around her shoulders, Matt led her past the table, bent and blew out the one candle that sputtered, and headed for the living room with Lucy in tow. "Good. Let's sit for a while. I have something for you."

He reached the couch and dropped down into the cushiony softness, pulling her along with him. Lucy flopped across his lap and nuzzled his neck with a giggle when Mr. Pibbs meowed loudly and jumped to the floor.

Matt closed his eyes, enjoying the way her lips moved across his neck. "Don't you want your present?" He thought about the gold bracelet sitting in a small box in his shirt pocket.

Her hand fluttered across his broad chest. "Don't you want yours?" Her fingers traveled over the buttons of his shirt, opening them one by one. One quick tug, and his shirttails were on the outside of his pants.

Matt licked his lips. "What about supper? Don't you want to eat first?"

She nodded her head. "Uh-huh. That's exactly what I plan to do." She smiled and worked his zipper down, reached inside the slit of his briefs, and pulled his erection free. "I plan to have my appetizer right now. I don't get very many chances to do this since we eat out all the time. My house, Matt. My rules."

Raising his palms in the air, he shrugged with a smile. "What can I say when my girlfriend's hungry?"

Resting his head back against the cushion, Matt closed his eyes, knowing what was coming and tried to control his breathing because of it. Lucy's fingers stroked the length of his cock. Each time she slid her hand upwards, she applied light pressure, teasing him with the milking motion she knew he loved. Matt growled in his throat, but kept his eyes closed and his hips still.

A whisper of a kiss against his breast increased the tempo of his heart rate slightly, and then she swirled her tongue around one erect nipple. Placing her mouth directly over it, she sucked with force. Matt's penis bobbed beneath her fingers in response.

"Matt?"

"Hmmm?"

"I want you to do this to me tonight. I want you to suck on my nipples."

"Anything you want, Luce. Just don't stop."

"I don't plan to."

Her tongue left a moist path across his other breast, and then slid sensuously down and over the ripples of his hard stomach as she slid from the couch to kneel between his legs. Small feathery kisses were pressed sporadically down the line of wiry hair that stretched from his navel to his groin.

"Keep your eyes closed, Matt. But lift your hips so I can slide your pants off."

He rose slightly and felt the material of both his pants and boxers slide past his ankles. Listening intently, the rustle of clothes falling to the ground met his ears before she urged his hips closer to the edge of the couch. "Did you just take your clothes off?"

"Don't peek." A hand touched his knee, sliding slowly up between his legs. Matt's cock throbbed in response, but the light touch was gone in a flash. A hand on each of his knees replaced her previous touch as she spread his legs wider. "I'm licking my lips, Matt. I'm moistening them so they can slide easily down your cock."

"Jesus, Lucy—"His chest expanded with each deep breath he took.

He jerked forward when her tongue flicked at the droplet of moisture that clung to the tip of his cock.

"God, Lucy. Suck me—don't wait any longer."

The warm breath from her mouth heated the side of his penis when a tiny giggle bubbled in her throat. "But didn't you tell me that anticipation is half the fun?"

He grabbed her head between his hands, forced her mouth over his throbbing cock, and pumped his hips. Lucy's swirling tongue around the length would have buckled his knees if he weren't already in a sitting position.

She lapped, nipped, and sucked as her head bounced up and down. Wiggling her hand between them, she cupped his balls and stroked them gently until they tightened, then replaced her fingers with her mouth, rolling one testicle with her tongue.

Matt's hands dropped limply to the soft cushion as she worked him into a near encompassing heat that would end with him coming if he didn't pull his cock from her seeking mouth. His eyes snapped open, dark with desire as she continued to suck on him.

He pushed her head back, grabbed her shoulders, and gently forced her to her hands and knees. Matt dropped behind her and rammed his throbbing penis into her pussy. She was hot, wet, and ready for his entry.

Slamming against her, Matt watched her whip her hair back and brace her body to meet each hard thrust eagerly. It was a contest of who could hold out the longest. Their tumultuous actions caused his cock to slip out of her dripping pussy. Matt grabbed his penis, repositioned his knees and jammed into her ass.

Lucy grunted her excitement and met him with excited driving force. She craved the feeling of him even deeper inside her and backed up against his body.

They came at the same time; the long deep strokes created waves that shook them; rocked them with the intensity of whirling physical sensations.

Lucy's head dropped to the carpeted floor. Matt remained impaled inside her as he leaned forward, cupped her breasts tenderly, and kissed her perspiring back. A moment later, he withdrew from her body, helped her from her knees to lie on her stomach, and rolled to the carpet beside her. His chest rose and fell as he tried to regain some semblance of normal breathing. Lucy's panting voice echoed in his ears.

"That was incredible…"

His hand reached out to touch her arm. "You're like no one I know. No woman has ever made me feel the way you do."

Lucy reached out a tentative finger and traced the line of his jaw. "Matt?"

He turned his head to stare into her eyes.

"Did you mean that?"

"Mean what?"

"That I'm the only woman that ever made you feel the way you do."

"Where are you going with this, Lucy?"

Her fingers raveled their way through the thick hair on his chest. "What about the woman you lived with for so long."

Matt closed his eyes for a moment. No matter how he treated her, it always came back to his old flame, Steph. *The guy from Lucy's past must have really done a number on her.* She continually worried and made comments that Matt's past would come back to haunt their relationship and he would disappear. It was the one thing she feared most.

"How many times have I told you that I'm with you now — that you make me happy and that Steph is totally out of my life?" He turned to catch the look of disquiet etched on her face—that same look she always tried to hide when this discussion came up between the two of them—a discussion that happened far too often because of her insecurities.

"I know you tell me, but so did the guy I was with. I'm sorry, Matt, but I don't want to lose you." She took his hand in hers as she stared at him and decided to go for it. "I love you, Matt."

He simply stared as his lips silently parted.

Lucy swallowed and waited a moment longer for him to respond. When he didn't, she scurried to sit up and get away from him, but he tightened his fingers on hers to restrain her from standing.

Nervously, she ran her hand through her tumbled tresses and refused to look at him. "I should get dressed and get supper ready." She tried to shake her arm loose, embarrassed that she had blurted out her feelings. Obviously, Matt wasn't ready to take that step, no matter the intense sex they had just experienced and his repeated promises that he wasn't going anywhere.

"Come here, Lucy." He pulled her down and threw a muscular leg across her thighs to keep her from leaving. His fingers brushed red strands of wavy hair from her damp cheek. A thumb played about her full lips. "Are you crying?"

"Absolutely not." And another tear escaped to fall across her cheek.

"What you just said. Did you mean it?"

Her eyes closed for a moment, she swallowed to gain her composure, and then she stared back into the blue ones wavering above her. "I didn't mean to put you on the spot. It's okay if you don't love me. I'm just happy that you're here now and—"

A rumble built in his chest and soon a happy laugh escaped his lips as she continued to explain away her declaration. His head shook slowly as he lowered his mouth and kissed her deeply. "Lucy, Lucy…Lucy. You are one in a million. If you'd just shut up for a moment, you'd let me tell you that I'm not going to leave; you'd give me the chance to tell you how much I love you."

A happy squeal from her lips preceded her wrapping her arms around his neck and using her body to force him onto his back. She dropped kisses all over his laughing mouth and straddled him until Matt held her head still and tenderly kissed her into quiet submission.

* * * * *

They sat at her small dining table, having finished with dinner and talked about taking a small vacation. Both agreed that their declarations of love definitely moved their relationship further. Both wanted to celebrate the fact with a special long weekend. Lucy's new bracelet twinkled in the candlelight.

"I don't think Frank will give me any time off until after the Fourth of July. This is a busy time at the café. Plus, I already asked him for next weekend off—something I wanted to discuss with you."

A smile of complete contentment widened his mouth as he filled her wine glass. "Shoot. What do you want to discuss?"

Her finger circled the rim of her goblet. "I asked for next Friday off because it's my ten-year class reunion. I was hoping you would go with me."

"Sure. Sounds like fun."

She set her glass down and stared in surprise. "No questions? Just sure?"

He shrugged and sipped his wine.

Lucy rocketed off the chair, rounded the table, and landed in his lap. When she finished kissing him, she hugged him tightly.

"Lucy, what's the big deal? I'd love to escort you if you'll have me. It'll be fun to meet friends from your past."

She cupped his jaw and forced the pained smile to stay on her lips. "That's just the thing. High school wasn't a very pleasant experience. I was a little overweight and was made fun of."

Matt's heart sank; he hated to think of Lucy being hurt in any way. It was easy to see that the past still bothered her. She had absolutely no confidence when it came to the past — whether it was hers or his.

"You don't understand how important it is for me to show you off to all those lunkhead girls who always thought I wasn't good enough to find someone as handsome as you."

"Ohhh, so that's it. I'm the boy-toy on your arm to make everyone jealous?"

"I admit I'm guilty as charged. Does that bother you?"

"Hell no! We'll give 'em one helluva show that will keep those women's panties wet with jealousy and dreaming about what it would be like to screw someone like me!"

She playfully slapped him. "I think I just discovered the egotistical side of you that's been hiding since we met." Her eyes turned serious. "Thank you, Matt. I know it's childish, but those girls were so mean to me in high school. I never really had a special friend because they ostracized me and never quite allowed me in. I wasn't even going to go until I met you."

He drew her mouth close to hers. "Well, you did meet me. You did make me fall in love with you, and we'll be sure that every bitch at the reunion knows it."

Chapter Six: The Switch

Someone knocked on the trailer's door. Matt pushed his chair out from the desk with an exasperated sigh. He'd been working on a blueprint revision since arriving at work early that morning. The constant interruptions found him a lot further from completing his project than he wanted to be, and he needed to get home soon, shower, and pick up Lucy for her reunion by 6:00. It was all she had talked about, and he wanted to make this night one to remember.

"Come on in!" he hollered irritably over his shoulder. "It's open!" The door creaked behind him. "So, what the hell is it now?" He turned in his chair. "What the hell! Jake!" He bounded from the chair and gathered his twin brother into a bear hug. Each man could have been hugging his own reflection in the mirror. They were the same height, possessed the same muscular physique and facial features, and one's voice could easily be mistaken for the other.

"Good to see you, Matt." Jake slapped his brother's back. "Where in hell have you been? I've been trying to reach you all week."

"Nothing has happened in Milwaukee, has it?"

"Hell, no," Jake shook his head, "but you had better sit down." He watched Matt drop into the desk chair with an instant wary look on his face.

Jake strolled to a ratty couch, eyed it as if wondering if he should sit or not, then made the decision to perch on the edge. "Chrissakes, Matt, we make enough money that you could splurge on some better furniture. Dad would have a heart attack if he knew you were entertaining prospective customers in a shack like this."

"I never bring anyone in here except the workers for internal meetings. If I'm bidding, I make sure I wine and dine them someplace fancy. Don't you ever look at the expense reports?"

Jake laughed and it hit Matt once more how the two of them sounded alike. Even he could hear it.

"I trust my partner. You've got this company going in the right direction, Matt. We're making lots of money—we must because I get a check every two weeks that curls my toes."

Matt shook off his brother's cavalier attitude. Jake was as sharp as they came. He couldn't have found a better business partner to run the company their father had started. He also was acutely aware that Jake knew where every penny went.

"All right, what's up?" Matt crossed his arms over his broad chest and waited. "It must be something if you drove all the way up here. Or did you fly?"

Jake rested his elbow on his knees, clasped his hands, and stared across the room. "Stephanie is in the car."

Matt bounded from his chair a second time, strode to the window, and peered out to see his horrible past sitting presently in his brother's new red pickup. He spun on a booted heel and glared at Jake. "What the fuck were you thinking to bring her up here? Now she knows where I am. I broke it off finally and managed to figure out a way to disappear. Fuck you, Jake, for your goddamned stupidity!"

"Whoa, whoa, whoa! I more or less saved your ass yesterday!" Jake was now on his feet. "Stephanie managed to talk one of the secretaries into letting her know what site you were working at. I dragged her damn ass right out of her car at the last minute. She was all packed and on her way north to raise hell with you for disappearing. You can thank me, Mr. Bigshot, for talking her out of it for the moment. Knowing that she was going to show up sooner or later and bug-start another scene, I took it upon myself to ride up with her and play referee. I've been calling you for the last twenty-four hours to let you know. Don't you ever check your answering machine? What?" He had seen a flash of something pass through his brother's face, and then instantly disappear. "Do you have some little chippie that you were fucking last night? I called the apartment at least six times!" His blue eyes settled on the phone that lay on the table—unplugged. "I see why I couldn't get you all day."

Matt followed his brother's gaze. "I've been so damned busy, that I unplugged it so I could get some work done. I'm sorry, Jake, for shouting. That woman out there brings out the worst in me." His mind was already racing as he glanced at the clock. It was 4:00. He was going to have to get rid of her quickly. There was no way he was going to screw up Lucy's night—not when it was so important to her. He ran both hands through his thick hair. "What the hell does she want?"

Jake joined his brother at the window. Stephanie sat in the truck, touching up her lipstick and fluffing her platinum blonde hair. "How in hell did you spend four years with that woman? She drove me nuts on the way up here."

"You didn't answer me. What the fuck does she want?"

"Money. Lots of it."

"You could have done that. What else?"

"I imagine she wants you to squirm. She told me on the way up here that she wants you to take her to dinner and write out a check. She's a bitch all right. In her sick mind, she thinks she'll be making you miserable one more time. Then she plans to walk away."

"Well, fuck her. I have plans tonight, and I won't break them. Someone is depending on me for something." His shoulders dropped in a heavy sigh as he watched Stephanie alight from the truck and glance around the parking lot. "Wait here. I'm going out there." He took three steps in the direction of the door, before hesitating in front of the desk. Matt turned, yanked open a drawer and pulled out his checkbook. The door almost came off the hinges when he slammed it against the wall and walked stiffly outside.

Stephanie turned slowly with a sour smile on her powdered face. She waited until Matt stopped a few feet away. "Well, hello, Matthew. Long time, no see."

"What the hell are you doing here? I told you four months ago that it was over. In fact, I've told you that since last Christmas. We're spinning our wheels to discuss it anymore. You want money, Steph? Fine. Name your price. Just take it and get out of my life."

Her features drew tight. "I'm not letting you off that easy. I plan to spend the evening with you. After all, I've been looking for you for the last couple of months. You can at least show me the courtesy of buying me dinner. I have a list of things that I need paid off. I have no job, so I imagine we can talk about some maintenance also."

"We were never married, Steph. I put up with your bullshit long enough. You've got five minutes to decide how much you need. I'll write you a check, and then you can take Jake's truck for all I care and leave."

The woman ducked around him and headed for the steps to the trailer.

"Stephanie. You're not welcome in there. Any business we have can be done right here."

She glanced over her shoulder and continued up the stairs and through the open doorway. Matt stomped after her. When he entered the trailer, Jake stood, observed both their expressions, and sighed. "I'll just wait outside."

As the door closed, Stephanie dug in bag, pulled out a cigarette, and blew a stream of smoke across the room a moment later. She smiled succinctly. "It's amazing how the two of you could be the same person. I thought he was you a couple times back in Milwaukee."

"Get to the point." Matt stood with his fists clenched. woman had made his life miserable. It wasn't that way i beginning, though. There was a time he actually thought l in love with her. He mentally shook his head. It had ɡ wrong a few years back. Steph had a nervous breakdown and was never the same. In fact, she seemed to get crazier as the months passed. A flash of their sick relationship trickled through his mind. He had to get rid of her. Lucy was waiting. "How much do you want?"

Stephanie crossed the room and glanced up into his rigid features. "Two hundred thousand should do." She enjoyed the look of complete shock on his face. "Oh, don't look so surprised. It's been a tough three months since you ran away."

"I didn't run away. I'm trying to run a business."

Stephanie tried a different tack. Her hand reached up to caress his chest. "We used to be so good together. In fact..." her hand slid down the front of his body to rest on his crotch. "I wouldn't mind one last fuck before—"

Matt grabbed her hand and flung it away. "And put up with you telling me how much you hate me when I'm riding you? You're a sick bitch, Steph. One minute you were begging me for it, getting me all riled up. As soon as I put my dick in you, you screamed you hated me."

Her face pinched with instant disgust. "I want my money, and I want you to take me to dinner. I'm not leaving until that happens."

"I've got plans tonight. In fact, I need to get out of here as soon as possible. And I think I've changed my mind. You had plenty access to my checkbook when we were together. We're not an item anymore, and I'm done paying for your frivolous ways any longer."

Her jaw set stubbornly. "I could give a shit about your ns. I've been miserable since you left me. If you don't give me t I want, I'll never leave you alone. You thought I was a before, just wait." Her slim brows arched over her g eyes. "What are your plans, Matt? Do you have some ch you're fucking these days?" She saw the flash of p his eyes. "That's it. You've found someone that will your demanding sexual ways, haven't you."

"Shut up, Steph."

"Ooo—she must spread her legs wide if you're not willing to talk about her. Maybe I'll have to look her up."

Matt ignored her comments and stalked to the desk, whipped the checkbook out of his pocket, and scribbled across the first check he flipped to. He turned and held out his arm. "Here's your money. That's all you're getting."

"If you don't spend the evening with me, I promise you'll be sorry." Her voice rose. "In fact, I have another proposition for you. Take me back to Milwaukee. Drive me there tonight, and I'll walk out of your life. You'll never see me again. I've been spending time with Nicky Damon. You remember him, don't you? As soon as I get back, we're heading out of state. This seed money," she snapped the check from his outstretched hand "will help us out until we can get settled."

"Jake can take you back. I have plans."

Her eyes scanned the check in her hand. He saw the instant anger blaze dangerously when she noted the amount. "One thousand dollars? That's all I was worth to you?" Steph's face pinched tighter as her anger built. "Let Jake take care of whatever needs to be done. No one can tell the two of you apart anyway. Take me home. It's the least you can do if you're not going to help me financially."

"No! I'm through with you."

Steph dropped to her knees and wrapped her arms around his thighs, instantly turning into a pathetic blubbering mass.

Even though Matt had been accustomed to her quick mood swings, her mental state still astounded him.

"Matthew, please! Just do this last thing for me and I promise, I'll walk out of your life. You'll never hear from me again. Please, I want you to drive me." She sobbed wildly, her body shaking as she clung to him.

"Jesus Christ, Steph." He picked her arms loose and hauled her up to sit her on the couch. She only wailed louder.

"Matthew, please! Just give me a ride home. I don't even want your damned money. It's Nicky who wants the money. I just needed to see you once more. I needed to say goodbye before I left for good!" Tears stained a path down her powered cheeks. Her eyes stared unblinkingly at him, and then turned dark as she waited for a response. "If you don't do what I ask, I'll make trouble for you in this town."

She was crazy. "What happened to you, Steph? What brought you to this point?" Matt almost felt sorry for her.

"I'll be fine," she choked out, "if you'll just bring me home. Not Jake—you. I promise, Matt, that you'll never see me again." She hiccupped as she worked to settle herself down.

"I can't, Steph. I've got my own life now and have plans."

The insane anger returned. "You'll be sorry. If you won't bring me back, then I'm staying here for the weekend." She wiggled the check before his face. "This isn't much, but it'll pay for a room until I can find the bitch you're fucking these days." Steph enjoyed how his face lost its ruddy hue. She was devious enough to know she'd hit on the one thing that might get him to bring her back to Milwaukee. She needed more time with him to try and bilk him of some additional money. "Wait until I tell her about all the times we fucked—how you always told me you loved me." She leaned slightly forward with an evil smile on her lips. "You've told her you love her, haven't you?" She watched his face closely. "Your expressions always gave you away. Did you know that? I was always able to tell exactly what you were thinking. I think I'll even let this person know that you and I are thinking of rekindling our relationship—that it was just a stupid mistake when we parted. You'll be sorry—I guarantee it."

Steph sat back, pulled out another cigarette, lit it and blew the smoke past his face. She saw the first stirrings of indecision in his eyes. "Make up your mind, Matt. Either you bring me home or I won't stop until I find the bitch and let her know what living with you was like—all four sweet fucking years of it."

Matt wanted to punch her. He didn't doubt for a second that she would accomplish what she threatened. He could handle her lies, but what about Lucy? Sweet Lucy whose biggest insecurity sat here in the same room with him, ready to do damage no matter the consequences.

"Wait here." He strode to the door, yanked it open again, and joined his brother who leaned against his truck.

"Doesn't sound like it's going too good in there."

"The bitch wants me to drive her back to Milwaukee tonight. Jake—I've got to get rid of her. I've met someone who is so damned special that it scares me. I don't want to screw it up by having her meet up with Stephanie. This is a small town. It wouldn't take long for her to start a whole bunch of trouble for me." Matt dropped his forehead to his arm where it rested on the truck box.

"So, do it. She talked about that on the way up. Matt, I'm sorry I showed up with her, but better she come with me than be causing you trouble on the sly. There was no way I could talk her out of staying in Milwaukee. She's nuts." Jake straightened. "How much did she want?"

"Two hundred thousand." Matt listened to the air whistle between his brother's lips. "It's worth every penny if she'll just disappear out of my life."

"That's extortion."

"That's a way to get rid of her for good. Fuck. I can easily afford it, but fuck her. I gave her a thousand."

"Want me to ride along? We can take my truck and you can fly back."

"You're not leaving. You gotta help me out with something."

"Okay. What is it?"

"You've got to go to a class reunion tonight with a great gal. In fact, you have to get your ass out of here, get to my apartment and change. You have to be me tonight."

"You're shitting me, right?"

"I'm dead serious. I met this woman. Her name is Lucy O'Malley and she's the sweetest thing I've ever held in my arms. The one thing she's worried about the entire time we've been together is me leaving her and going back to Steph. Lucy has a huge load of baggage as far as both our pasts go. Some asshole raked her heart over the coals and really fucked with her confidence. The kids in her high school did the same thing." He glanced at his brother. "I love her, Jake. She had a tough time in school and going to this reunion with a man on her arm is the only thing she's talked about. Steph is threatening to find her and fill her with bullshit if I don't bring her back home tonight. Shit!" He slammed his fist against the truck's box. "There's no way I'm going to ruin Lucy's night by not showing up, especially if I tell her that an old crazy girlfriend that I lived with for four years needs a ride to Milwaukee. Do you think she'd understand that?"

Jake shrugged, accompanying the gesture with a smile. "Probably not. I know I'd tell you to go fuck yourself."

"We used to do this and get away with it all the time. Just one night and then we'll switch back." He raked his hand through his thick hair. "If I don't get rid of Steph, who knows what the hell kind of trouble she'll make. I've seen the bitch in action, and I don't want Lucy to have to go through the shit I know will happen."

"You know, Matt, it might work. All right, give me details so I don't screw up. It's been years since we did the old switcheroo, but I think I'm looking forward to this. My life's been a little boring lately."

"Before we set this up, I want to tell you one thing. Lucy is hot blooded as hell. We've got quite a thing going."

Jake squinted into the sun and peered at his brother. "Are you telling me to keep my hands off of her?"

"You bet I am. I trust you, Jake. Just get her drunk enough to pass out so you don't end up in bed with her. I've shared everything I own with you my entire life, but Lucy is off limits." Matt dug in his pocket and pulled out his apartment key. "The clothes are casual. I've got pants and a shirt hanging in plastic in my bedroom closet. You've got to get to her house by six and drive to Morton. My cologne is in the bathroom cabinet. Lucy has long red hair and freckles on her nose."

Jake listened closely as his brother spoke specifics he would need to know.

"She's renovated Johnson's old place on the end of town. She loves to garden and she loves me."

"Lucky guy."

"Lucy works at one of the local cafes. Has for three years. That's when she moved to town from Morton. She had a boyfriend who broke her heart before that."

Jake winced. "Hope her new boyfriend doesn't do it again."

Matt's heart lurched. Suddenly, he wasn't sure. "Shit. Maybe we shouldn't do this. I don't like duping Lucy this way, but that bitch in there is threatening big trouble. Lucy doesn't deserve that."

The trailer door slammed open. A red-faced Stephanie appeared in the doorway. "Matt! Bring me home. I told you I would never bother you again! Please!" she started to cry again.

The two men exchanged glances.

Stephanie wailed louder. "If you don't, you'll be sorry!"

Jake clasped his brother's shoulder. "I'll make sure this works. You gotta get her out of here."

Chapter Seven: The Swap

Lucy trembled with excitement as she scurried around the kitchen, finding anything to do to keep her busy until Matt showed up. As childish as it was, she had waited for this night for ten years. By eight o'clock, her old classmates would be envious of her for the first time. The tables would finally be turned. With Matt by her side, Lucy felt she could accomplish anything.

Grabbing Mr. Pibbs' bag of hard cat food, she rushed across the kitchen to his bowl, and then swore when she fumbled the bag in her hands. A second later, it skidded across the floor, spewing small hard chunks across the clean linoleum. "Shit!" She opened a closet door, yanked out a broom and started to sweep furiously. Matt knew what she was like with her constant fumbling ways, but for some reason, Lucy felt it was important to maintain an air of calm before him tonight. If she didn't, he would tease her mercilessly throughout the evening.

It only took another minute to clean the floor, in between swipes at Mr. Pibbs with the broom as he tried to eat from the linoleum. She shoveled the cat food from the dustpan and into his bowl.

Lucy raced up the steps for one more check in the bathroom mirror. A flushed face and glowing eyes stared back at her. Lifting her chin slightly, she stopped long enough to study her reflection. Auburn hair shone in the late afternoon sun that streamed in the window, hanging in ringlets from where she had piled it atop her head. Her sleeveless one-piece sheath hugged her breasts, tapered around narrow hips, and clung to her slim thighs and round butt. Matt would be blown away tonight with the way she looked and so would those awful girls who had tormented her on a continual basis.

And when the reunion was done? Her nipples immediately puckered beneath the satiny material. The night would culminate with her being held in his passionate arms as he coaxed one thrill after another from her body.

The crunch of gravel beneath tire treads brought her to the window. He was here to pick her up!

* * * * *

Lucy skidded to a halt in the kitchen and nearly tipped over on her new platform shoes. Her brow dipped with confusion as she looked around. *Where is he?* Someone knocked on the front door and immediately interrupted her thoughts. "Well, what the heck…" Matt never knocked anymore; he simply came through the door and pulled her into his arms.

"Matt?" she called out as she reentered the living room. "What the heck are you doing?" He stood on the front porch with a small bouquet of flowers in his hand looking through the screen door. "Since when did you start knocking?" Her hand rested on the door handle as she smiled up. "Ooo—you sure look handsome!"

Jake did his best to hide the surprise in his eyes. Lucy was a knockout—not what he expected. The image of a carrot-topped head and matching freckles of a farm girl vanished into thin air. He should have listened closer to his brother. Jake's knuckles turned white as he gripped the flowers and continued to stare at the beauty before him, trying to figure out what to say.

Her hands drifted to her hips, she tilted her head, and jutted out her breasts.

Jake's breath left his lungs and whistled through his teeth.

"So, what's the deal here? Why are you standing out there?"

Jake shook away the mental cobwebs that had clouded his brain at the sight of her. "I...ah...figured this was a special night. I'm picking you up like a normal date would, instead of barging in like I own the place." *I'll kill that son of a bitch for not filling me in completely!* "Lucy, you're one of the sexiest ladies I've ever met. You look fantastic!" He remembered the flowers in his hand and quickly held them out. "These are for you."

She opened the door, grabbed his hand, and pulled him inside. Taking the flowers in one hand, she draped her other arm around his neck and urged his head down.

A bolt of electricity shot through his body when his mouth touched hers. Lucy ran her tongue between his lips. Jake could do nothing more than kiss her back. When his arms remained stiffly at his side, she broke the contact and immediate concern darkened her gaze.

She stared up. "Is something wrong?"

He shook his head. "No, why?"

Her arm dropped from his neck. "You seem a little distant. It's as if you're kissing a stranger." Her previous excitement dimmed as her earlier self-confidence disappeared. "Have you changed your mind about tonight?"

Think, Jake! "It's just that...it's just the way you look tonight. You're absolutely beautiful—just when I thought you couldn't get any better. You blow me away." Her sudden smile assured him he had said the correct thing.

Her palm drifted to his chest. "Then let's start the night over. Kiss me, Matt." She brushed her breasts against his chest and molded herself to the long line of his body—and fit perfectly.

It's only in the name of brotherly love... Jake's hands slid around her trim waist as he pulled her into his embrace, lowered his mouth, and kissed her for all he was worth. Lucy's lips were moist and welcoming. The flowers floated to the floor. An arm slid around his waist as she caressed his ass and pulled him closer. The quiet moan in the back of her throat gave him an instant hard-on, but his eyes snapped open when her hand trailed to his crotch and cupped his balls gently. Then she kissed his throat and played with the wavy hair at the back of his neck.

"I wish I had time to take care of this..." her hand found the outline of his erection through his pants and stroked it with promise. "You're always so ready for me."

Jake was glad she couldn't see his face. *What the hell kind of intense relationship does he have with her?* "Me, too...but...don't you think we should get going? Besides, I wouldn't want to mess one beautiful strand of hair on your head. You're going to knock them dead tonight."

She positively glowed from his compliments when she leaned back in his embrace. Her fingers stroked his jaw tenderly. "How was I so lucky to find you? I love you so much, Matt."

Jake quickly pulled her close again and whispered beside her ear. "Me, too. I love you, Luce." As soon as the words left his mouth, he wondered if his brother had told her that yet.

"I know you do, but thank you for telling me that all the time."

Jake looked heavenward over her shoulder and mouthed a silent thank you to his brother. He had said the right thing. "Well, babe, are you ready to go?"

✶ ✶ ✶ ✶ ✶

Lucy and Jake walked hand in hand up the lighted sidewalk of the Morton Country Club. Her fingers tightened around his as they approached the door. Jake squeezed them to give her confidence. It amazed him how much he had learned about her on the twenty-minute drive down. High school was a horrible experience for her, being one of those kids who were never included in any of the special activities. All she could talk about was that maybe she had made a mistake coming here. The nasty girls from her past still had the ability to turn her stomach inside out. Her palms were perspiring, and she stated more than once that her stomach was in knots.

Jake was already determined to make this night the best possible and not because of his brother's wish—he simply wanted to do it for her. Lucy was a fantastic lady. It was easy to see she was pure of heart and totally in love with Matt. His brother was one lucky guy. Jake's earlier misgivings vanished. They had done the right thing to keep Steph from messing with this fine woman.

Jake's insides jumped thinking about the two of them. Lucy's babbling on the way down had also confirmed that the two of them had one hot sexual relationship. When she wasn't worrying about what everyone would think of her, she had teased Jake with promises of how the night would end. *Shit, I'm going to have to get her drunker than a skunk.* He already knew that he was going to have a helluva time keeping his hands off her.

They entered the building and started up the stairs to the ballroom. Suddenly, Lucy tripped on the third step and would have gone flying if he hadn't caught her. Grabbing her firm waist, Jake steadied her on her feet.

"That was a close one!"

Lucy straightened her dress around her hips and took a deep breath—one that stretched her bodice to the limit.

Jake immediately matched her breath with one of his own.

"Don't tease me, Matt. I'm trying so hard to stay calm." Blinking back the tears that sparkled in her eyes, she did a quick scan of the stairway. "No one saw me, did they?"

"Not a soul in sight. Just hang onto my arm, Luce. We'll show those bitches you're one heck of a lady."

She grasped his arm, hugged it closely, and sent him a smile that melted his heart. "Thank you. Thank you for being here with me tonight and understanding my dilemma."

The sight of her trusting eyes thanking him, making him feel like her savior, made him feel like a heel and caused the damned misgivings to return. As he stood beside her, it was a monumental effort to not blurt out the truth. Already, he hated the idea of duping her. But he had promised Matt and understood why his brother wanted to protect her.

Lucy had a way of doing that. Stephanie was one little issue that needed to be buried, and she would be gone from Matt's life tonight. Lucy shouldn't have to worry about it. If Lucy belonged to him, he would have done the same thing—anything so as not to hurt this wonderful woman.

He tucked her hand more firmly around his arm, patted it with his palm, and smiled down. "Let's go wow them."

* * * * *

And wow them they did. Many pairs of eyes—both male and female—followed them to wonder at the transformation of Lucy O'Malley and whom the handsome, dark stranger was.

Jake was the perfect escort. By the time they purchased their first drinks, a petite blonde approached them where they stood by the end of the bar.

"Lucy?" Her false smile widened. "Lucy O'Malley? Is that really you?" Her eyes did a quick once over the surprisingly changed schoolmate, and then turned to Jake with a huge, red-lipped grin. "And who is this?"

"Hello, Shirley. I haven't seen you since high school."

It was all Shirley could do to drag her gaze from the smiling Jake and back to Lucy. "Yes, it has been a long time." Immediately, she checked out Jake again. "Is this your husband?"

"No, this is a good friend of mine, Matt Diamond. Matt, this is Shirley Bernard."

Jake snaked his arm around Lucy's shoulder and gave it a squeeze before he extended a hand to take the drooling woman's palm. He'd been around her type many times before. It was easy to see she could give a shit less about Lucy. "Nice to meet you, Shirley."

"Likewise. And my name is Shirley *Jenkins.* I married after college, but it didn't last. I'm *single* now, but never took back my maiden name," she pouted out with a smile, and then gripped his fingers, letting him know she was undeniably interested.

All right, that's enough of this. He withdrew his hand. "Lucy and I met this year." He turned his head, noticed the clenched smile on her face, and decided to do something about it. "She's changed my life." He brushed Lucy's flushed cheek with a tender kiss, rubbed his fingers softly over her bare shoulder, and was rewarded with a knowing smile. "And contrary to what she said, we're definitely more than just friends." He continued to stare at the woman curled into his arm—not because he was playing the part anymore, but because her lips parted slightly as she gazed up, making him want to dip his head and kiss her passionately.

Shirley cleared her throat to gain their attention, wishing just once that a man would look at her that way, would strip her naked with just a simple glance.

Lucy's slim brow arched over one eye when she was finally able to drag her gaze from Jake and return her attention to the rigid woman standing with them. "Sorry about that. Matt has a way of making me forget what I'm doing." She lifted her drink to her mouth to hide her smile when Shirley's jaw clenched in anger.

Before the woman could say anything else, Jake clasped Lucy's free hand. "Say, sexy lady, how about we find a place to sit? A nice, cozy spot close to the dance floor? I plan to hold you in my arms all night." He nuzzled the sweet-smelling spot below her ear, and then forced his eyes back to Lucy's old classmate. "Maybe we'll have a chance to chat later, Shirley. Nice meeting you."

Shirley stared in shock when he whisked Lucy past her and across the floor. By the time the two found a table, they both shook with strangled laughter. Jake pulled out a chair, waited for Lucy to sit, and quickly grabbed another and pulled it close.

Lucy took a sip of her drink, choked slightly as she tried not to snort out her glee, and shook her head. "You are a horrible man, but thank you, thank you, thank you! That was the best dressing down I ever saw. That little episode was worth all the years of torment she threw my way."

Jake lifted her hand and kissed the back of it. "I meant every word. You are a sexy lady, you have changed my life, and I'm glad we're more than friends." A flash of consciousness jabbed him. He hoped he wouldn't regret saying those words later on tonight. Lucy was not his; she belonged to Matt.

The smile left her lips. Lucy leaned into him, cupped his jaw lightly, and kissed his lips softly. "So am I. I love you, Matt. You make me the happiest woman in the world. How was I so lucky?"

Jake was thankful that the room was crowded with people, or he would have pulled her close and kissed her full lips until she fainted. It was going to be a rough night. "That's the second time you've said that tonight."

"What?"

"Trying to figure out why you were so lucky to find me. Lucy, look around. There isn't a man here who hasn't ogled you at least once. I'm the lucky one."

She sat back and glanced innocently around the ballroom. "What are you talking about? No one is watching me. I've never been one of those girls who attract a lot of attention. I'm not a Shirley Jenkins with her petite body, perfect nails, and blonde hair."

Jake couldn't help himself. He leaned forward, breathed in the scent of her perfume, and kissed her neck just above the collarbone. "I'm glad you're not. Otherwise, I wouldn't be sitting here with the prettiest girl in the room. When I look at you, I know exactly what I'm getting. You're honest, ego-free, and sincere in everything you do."

And Jake meant it. He would give anything to find someone like Lucy to spend the rest of his life with.

"Excuse me, sir. Would you like another drink?" The waiter was a godsend.

The sudden appearance of the man shook Jake from his dream-like state as he stared into Lucy's shimmering eyes. He had to remember that he was simply saving his brother's ass tonight; he had to remember that Lucy wasn't really his. "Yeah, we'll take two more Manhattans. In fact, bring a double round. It's going to be a long night." He grabbed his glass, drained the contents, and set his glass on the man's tray.

As the waiter walked away, Lucy shook her head. "So, who's going to drive home? I'll guarantee you that it won't be me if you keep shoving these strong drinks down my throat. I'm not used to having a whole lot of liquor."

"Don't you worry about it. This is your night. You drink, have fun, and I'll get you home with no trouble." The band struck up a jitterbug as he spoke. "Hey, you want to dance?"

Her face lit up. "I'd love to!" As he took her hand and stood, she laughed at his eagerness. "I thought you said you didn't care much for dancing?"

Shit. She's right. Matt always prefers to sit and watch the crowd. "Well, tonight's a special occasion! We've got some crowd-working to do. Let's not forget that we're going to make them green with envy!"

He pulled Lucy onto the dance floor that was quickly filling with couples, took one hand in his, and wrapped the other around her tiny waist. Lucy squealed her delight when his feet started to move to the beat.

When they weren't dancing, they were visiting with the many classmates who made their way to the couple's table. Jake kept Lucy's glass filled as she laughed merrily with more than one boy from her class. As snotty as some of the women could be, he was amazed that not once did Lucy return a barbed comment. She was congenial and having the time of her life.

Soon, the pointed jabs disappeared and were replaced by questions of interest as far as where she worked, what had happened in her life over the last ten years, and if she would be interested in keeping in touch in the future.

The band returned to the stage after a short break. As soon as Jake heard the strains of "The Way You Look Tonight", he tossed away his earlier resolve not to dance a slow song with Lucy. He stood, took a sip of his drink, and tapped her on the shoulder as she giggled with three girls from her past. Four sets of eyes glanced up. "Excuse me, ladies. But I've got the sudden urge to steal this beautiful woman out to the dance floor." Audible sighs were heard around the table when Lucy stood and was led to the middle of the room.

Lucy giggled when his arms wrapped protectively around her. She flung her hands around his neck and swayed to the music. "I think that was the night's final coup." She hiccupped and giggled again. "Did you hear them sigh? They watched us all the way out to the floor."

Jake stared at her mouth. "I didn't ask you to dance because of our plan. I wanted to hold you in my arms and feel your body next to mine."

"Oh, Matt..." she laid her head against his chest and sighed deeply as they moved slowly across the floor. "I feel like Cinderella."

He pulled her closer, his heart jumping when her body molded to his. "You're much prettier than Cinderella." Jake's palm slid down her arm until he found her hand. He held it to his lips, kissed it, then tucked her fingers close to his heart as they swayed to the soft strains.

Lucy's head fell back as she stared up. Her tongue darted innocently over her bottom lip as she smiled dreamily. "I love this song. I'll never listen to it again without thinking of you holding me in your arms." Her eyelids fluttered. "Oooo—I think I'm drunk." She giggled again. "Am I drunk, Matt?"

A chuckle rumbled in his throat. "Yes, Lucy, I think you are."

"Hmmm…what if I pass out before we can make love tonight?"

Jake almost lost his footing, but recovered quickly. "So, you pass out knowing you had the most wonderful night of your life in a long time." The thought of leaving her alone in her house, though, cut him to the quick. He wanted Lucy more than any other woman. But, she wasn't his. She belonged to Matt.

Lucy rubbed her cheek against his shoulder, sighing with contentment. "Oh, I don't think so, Mr. Diamond. No night is complete until you take my body and do whatever you want with it."

Jake's lids slammed shut above her head. The night was nearly over. He had to make sure she drank enough to pass out—even if he had to buy a bottle for her to drink once they got home, or he was doomed.

Chapter Eight: A Plan Gone Wrong

Thirty minutes later, the ballroom lights glared brightly and people hugged one another goodbye. Lucy received her fair share as she wobbled around on her platform shoes, laughing and throwing kisses. Jake held her arm so she wouldn't tip over. He was pretty certain that he would be able to get to his brother's apartment without breaking his trust. He had pumped drinks into Lucy all night. Surely it was going to hit her and hit her hard soon. What he hoped would happen is that she would close her eyes and be out until morning. Jake was just about stretched to the level of no return. The constant presence of her warm, shapely body pressing up against him was beginning to eat at his restraint.

He managed to get her down the steps and out to the parking lot, having to steady her three separate times as she stumbled beneath his arm. Jake propped a giggling Lucy against the side of Matt's Suburban, kept one hand on her shoulder for good measure so she didn't end up face down, and dug for his keys. He would be free in about twenty-five minutes by his calculations. It was like a race in his head now to get her home and away from him.

The lock clicked open on the passenger side. Lucy grabbed his arm and pulled him towards her. "Hey, sexy man—give me a kiss."

Rather than argue with her, Jake brushed his lips against her waiting mouth, opened the passenger door, and then made to help her onto the seat. Lucy's fingers stopped him as they curled in the material of his shirt and yanked him close. "I know you can do better than that. Kiss me." She pulled his mouth down to hers, forcing his lips open to receive her tongue.

"Luce...we should..." he mumbled against her mouth and tried not to respond.

Her fingers flailed to find his hand at his side and, once she found it, she pressed it firmly between her legs a moment later. Somewhere in the fog of alcohol, Jake's groan was heard in her hazy mind. The sound spurred her on. "I don't want to wait until we get home. Dragging her hemline up, she found his hand again by traveling down the bulging length of his arm, and held his palm against her. The only thing that separated his hand from the heat of her pussy was a thin layer of silk. Jake's heart thudded. His fingers burned to be inside her. But he couldn't. He pulled the hem of her dress back over a silky thigh.

"Come on, Lucy. Let's get in the truck. There are too many people who might see us."

She wiggled, pulled him closer, and pleaded against his lips. "God, I want you to fuck me. At least kiss me, Matt. Don't make me wait for that."

There was nothing he could do but kiss her. *Just this – I need to taste her just once...* He yanked her to his chest and lowered his lips. Lucy's tongue darted into his mouth, urging him to return the same. Jake's tongue swirled against hers. She tasted like fine brandy, sweet...womanly. A bare leg wrapped around his outer thigh. *Christ...* His hand found a swollen breast. Jake longed to free it and suck her nipple until she screamed. *I want to fuck you, Lucy...* He ground his erection against her and was rewarded with an answering thrust.

"Hey, you two! Take it home!"

Jake jumped back and steadied Lucy against the side of the truck. Whoever yelled, laughed into the darkness of the night and faded away amongst giggles of the partner who walked with him. The interruption was like a cold blast of water.

Lucy's hand covered her lips. She hiccupped again, and then giggled. "Oops! Looks like someone was watching us." She unceremoniously pushed herself away from the vehicle and tottered on the platform shoes. "Screw these shoes." She kicked one leg, the shoe went flying, and Jake saved her from tumbling to the pavement, before letting go of her as if he was burned. Lucy never even noticed. The other shoe followed as she struggled to keep her balance.

Lucy stared down at her bare toes, wiggled them, then glanced up, taking a moment longer than usual to settle her gaze on Jake. "That was a stup…" a burp sounded in the back of her throat. "…stupendous kiss." A crooked smile curved her mouth. "You know what, Matt? You're awful quiet. Oops." A slender hand clutched her forehead. "I think I better sit down. Things are kinda spinnin'."

Jake jumped forward when she fell back against the truck and started to slide down the side of the vehicle. He grabbed her limp arm, thankful that her many drinks were finally hitting her brain, and lifted her against his chest. A moment later, he muscled her into the front passenger seat.

"Wheeeeeeee!" she hiccupped as her body floated through the air. "Oh…I don't think we should do that again." She grabbed Jake's arm to stop the spinning as he belted her in.

He couldn't help but grin at the sorry state she was in. "You got that right." He was sure she was talking about being lifted into the truck—not the earlier embrace he was now berating himself for. Jake wasn't the sort of man to take advantage of any woman—especially his brother's girlfriend—but Lucy affected him like no other. "Close your eyes and go to sleep, Luce. I'll have you home in no time."

"Okay," she mumbled when her head slumped back.

Jake closed her door, walked to the back of the Suburban, and leaned against the tailgate. He breathed deeply to clear his head and ran both hands through the dark hair at his temples. "Shit—she thinks her head is spinning." He waited until his erection had completely disappeared before he stood and walked around to his door. As quietly and quickly as possible, he slid into the driver's seat in order to get the door shut and the interior light dimmed.

He thought he had everything licked until he inserted the key and started the engine.

"Are we home?"

Jake cursed silently. "Nope. Why don't you just rest your head? I'll let you know when we get there." Slamming the vehicle in reverse, he backed out of his spot. Lucy's head bobbed when he switched to Drive, headed out of the parking lot onto the highway, and turned north.

"Wow. How many drinks did I have tonight?"

"Plenty." Jake sighed wearily, realizing Lucy could hold her booze better than most men, even if she didn't know it.

She turned her head, rested a cheek against the seat, and stared, her eyes warm and glowing with love. "Thank you for tonight. I had so much fun."

"My pleasure." He smiled. "You were quite a hit."

A soft sigh left her mouth. "That's because of you. I love you."

Jake swallowed, afraid to look at her. "I love you, too." He reached out and squeezed her hand, wishing the moment were real. Lucy was one heck of a woman. He heard the snap of her seatbelt as it was released and glanced in her direction. "What are you doing? You should be belted in, Lucy. It's late—there might be a lot of drunks on the road."

"Like me?" she giggled. A second later, she reached out a slender palm and lightly dropped it between his legs.

Jake grabbed her hand and gently pushed it away. "Come on, I'm driving. Why don't you sleep until we get to your place?" *Shit — please go to sleep!*

She slid across the bench seat, swung an arm over his shoulders, and nuzzled the spot below his neck. "I love how you smell."

His fingers gripped the steering wheel. *You smell Matt, not me...*

The top button of his shirt was already open. Lucy made sure the next two in line followed suit.

"Come on, Luce. I can't concentrate on driving when you're doing that."

Silently, she pulled his shirt from inside his pants, gave up on the buttons, and whisked her fingers beneath the cotton material and up the naked tautness of his firm belly to his chest. "But I know you'll like what I'm thinking."

His hand pinned her wrist against his chest beneath the shirt. Glancing sideways, he tried to keep one eye on the road as he searched her profile in the darkness. "Just what *are* you thinking?" He had to know. He had to hear what she would say. It would be something he could take with him when he and Matt switched back to their real identities. It would be his fantasy for the rest of his life.

"Let go of my hand," she whispered into his ear. She tugged once and waited for her wrist to be released.

Jake fought the battle of his life. Lucy had cast an unknowing spell over him with her womanly body, her perfect little freckled face, and her unconscious sex appeal from the moment he walked through her front door.

But she was Matt's woman. He and his brother had shared everything over the course of their entire lives. Twins did that. Whether it was a bike, a car, or the business they both now ran. But never, *never* had they shared the same woman.

Lucy tugged her captured wrist again to no avail. "What's the matter, Matt? I want you." She kissed his earlobe, and then swirled her tongue inside his ear. "I love you. I've never loved anyone like you in my life." Lucy sucked his neck and rubbed her breast against his bare arm. "You make me hot...you make me wet with desire...only you...only you can do that to me..."

"You don't understand."

"Yes I do. I understand that I'm drunk. I understand that you're driving. That's all you have to do..." Her hushed voice warmed his neck as she whispered softly and nipped him through his shirt. "I'll do the rest."

The hair stood on the back of Jake's neck. His erection throbbed against his zipper.

"Please, honey..." she wheedled, "I want to fuck you with my mouth...now...not twenty minutes from now. I want to suck you like I've never done before. Let me lick you...please."

"Jesus..." Jake hissed.

She shifted and pressed herself tightly against his arm. Lucy continued her assault. "My pussy is dripping just because of what I want to do to you." Her tongue licked slow, tortuous circles below his ear. "I can't wait to get home. Then you can fuck me. First...my pussy..." her tongue darted into his ear, "you can lick it," she sucked on his earlobe, "then you can fuck it...then I want your hard cock up my ass..."

Jake released her wrist and gripped the steering wheel with both hands. He couldn't fight the onslaught of her promises any longer. He couldn't fight his desire to experience what she promised.

Lucy smiled into the darkness. "You won't be sorry," she whispered louder as she withdrew her arm from around his neck. Her left hand joined the right one that was already working his zipper to free his cock.

Jake's jaw clenched as his eyes searched the road before him. He had to find a spot to pull over.

Lucy had his penis in her right hand and teased him with slow, tight strokes from the base of his shaft to the head of his cock. Jake could barely breath.

He cranked the wheel just in time to spin off the highway onto a deserted road. Lucy continued to play with his cock, knowing that he was trying to find a spot for them to park. She would wait until she had his full attention.

Jake made three corners, heading for a secluded spot he remembered as a kid. When he finally slammed the vehicle into park and cranked the key off, he was breathing like he'd run a race. Dragging Lucy into his arms, he kissed her passionately, in a state of mind that he would fuck her before he left this spot. He couldn't stop now.

Surprisingly, she had enough strength to break the embrace and push him backwards against the door. Lucy grasped the open waist of his pants. "Lift your hips. I want these pants off of you," she ordered with a firm look in her eye.

Jake used one arm on the back of the seat and the other on the steering wheel to lever himself upwards until she dragged his pants down past his knees. His boxers followed, freeing his cock to stand rigid for her view in the bright moonlight.

Lucy swept both articles of his clothing past his ankles, pulled his loafers off, and tossed the entire mess to the back seat. Her hands yanked Jake's knees further apart. She stared at his cock, brought her gaze to his waiting eyes, and then smiled before she licked her lips.

Lucy worked her hands across his inner thighs until she took his cock in both palms. She clamped on to his erection, bent forward, and licked the tip. She heard the intake of Matt's breath. The sound urged her on. She opened her lips, slid over the glistening tip, and took the entire length of him into her mouth.

Jake's head fell back as his mouth sagged open. He didn't think about Matt; he didn't think about the consequences. All he could feel was her hot tongue working the hole at the end of his cock and her hand gently massaging his balls. All he could think about was how hot he'd been for her the entire evening.

He'd never had a blowjob like this in his life. He started to pump against her mouth. Lucy lapped at him, and then worked her lips to the base of his cock. She rode his length with her tongue time and time again as the tempo of his hips increased.

Jake began to grunt. The knuckles of both hands turned white as he gripped at anything to keep his grinding going. Lucy slowly drew her mouth the length of him until she reached the end and sucked hard on the tip as she stroked him with her hand.

"Lucy…" he grunted, "I'm going to…"

"I want you to!" she mumbled against his cock and sucked harder.

Jake grabbed the back of her head. Long, tortuous strokes of his cock into her mouth brought him to a peak. Lucy's head bobbed ferociously. She sucked even harder until Jake lurched forward. Warm streams of cum spurted to the back of her throat. She swallowed, lapping at his tip as he emptied himself, and then lifted her head as she stroked him dry.

Jake lay weakly with his head against the window of the door. "That was…I can't even describe it." His trembling hand wiped the perspiration from his brow.

Lucy crawled up his chest and licked his nipple. "Now, it's my turn. I want you to fuck me all the ways I asked you to."

Jake pushed damp strands of hair behind her ears. Lucy's red hair was a riotous mess, but she looked wild and beautiful. "Right here? You want me to put the back seat down so you can be comfortable?"

"Let's go outside," she whispered conspiratorially. "You grab the blanket out of the back. I'll get undressed." She pushed away from him with her arms, flicked on the interior light overhead, and looked in the backseat. "Yup, it's still there." Turning her hot gaze back on Jake, she stopped short as she stared at his chest. Tentatively, she reached out, and her fingers touched a tiny raised scar on his breast, hiding within his chest hair just above the right nipple. "What's this? I've never noticed this scar before."

Shit! "It's just an old scar." He watched her eyes closely.

"I can't believe I've never seen it before. What happened?"

"It's just a dumb accident when I was a kid."

"And?"

"I slid out of a tree when I was a kid and received ten stitches for not being a very good climber. No big deal."

Her brow furrowed. "You would have thought I'd have seen that before."

She was going to study it closer, but Jake grabbed her shoulders and pulled her mouth to his, anything to get her mind off the childhood injury. His hands massaged her ass and pressed her body close.

Lucy immediately forgot about the scar. "Hmmm…let's go outside. I can't wait to feel you inside me." She moved to her door and had it popped open a second later.

Jake grabbed her wrist before she left the vehicle. "Just wait for me, Lucy. Don't take your clothes off until I can watch."

She kissed him. "You do love to watch me strip, don't you. I'm glad you don't get bored with it."

The prick of consciousness that hit him almost knocked the wind out of his lungs. It was Matt who loved to watch her strip. Jake had never seen her naked body, but there was no turning back. Somehow, this would work out, and Lucy would never know his and Matt's deceit. *Correction, you bastard. Your deceit. Matt never asked you to fuck her.*

"Hurry up. I'll wait for you outside." Lucy slid from the seat and disappeared into the darkness.

Jake closed his eyes for a second, took another deep breath, and left the truck. He grabbed a blanket from the back seat, took a second to shrug off his shirt, and rounded the Suburban as fast as he could. Lucy took his hand and weaved across the grass, heading for the shallow stream just off the road. Jake followed, loving how the moonlight turned her hair a dark shade of fire red.

They reached a grassy knoll. The moonlight cast a blue pallor across the landscape, making Jake feel as if he walked in a dream. He would have this one night with this fantastic woman, and then he would walk away, his secret deception hidden forever.

Jake shook out the blanket and smoothed it across the ground. Before he could turn, Lucy wrapped her arms around him from behind. Her cheek rubbed across the bare skin of his back. "We've never made love outside. This is a special night."

He turned and gathered her into his arms, lowered his mouth, and kissed Lucy before her words fed his guilt any further. "Strip for me, Lucy."

She stepped back. Her fingers threaded their way up the sides of her head. Lucy removed one pin after another until her thick hair cascaded down past her shoulders. It was easy for her to reach behind and find the zipper sitting low on her back.

Jake watched her arm lower, knowing that the dress was now open. His heart thundered.

Lucy slid the thin straps from her shoulders, exposing her breasts a moment later. She was braless beneath the garment. When the dress drifted to the grass-covered ground, she stood only in a black thong. Cupping her breasts for his enjoyment, she squeezed them together and played with her nipples. Swiveling to present her back to him, she watched him over her shoulder as she hooked the lace at her hips with her fingers, bent slightly forward, and drew her panties slowly down her long legs.

She turned for his inspection, a goddess standing in a shaft of moonlight, waiting to be made love to. Jake stepped forward, reached out, and caressed her heavy breasts with his hands. His knuckles rode lightly down past her rib cage. Seeking fingers trembled across her flat belly until they worked their way through the soft pubic hair at the apex of her legs.

Lucy grasped his shoulders as her head lolled back and spread her stance, opening herself for him.

Jake's eyelids closed when he ran a finger through her wet slit. Lucy flinched against his hand and ground forward. He shoved his finger firmly inside of her, cupped her ass with his other hand, and lifted her into the air, his upper arm supporting her back as she lay impaled in his arms.

"Oh..." her one throaty word excited him like nothing else ever had.

Jake forced her mouth open with his tongue and stroked his finger inside of her as her legs dangled from his firm grip.

"Oh, God..." she mumbled against his lips.

Jake set her gently on the blanket, kept his finger tightly inside of her pussy, and kneeled between her splayed legs. It was only when he leaned forward that he withdrew his finger to spread her lips wide for easy access to her clitoris. His tongue pressed against her body. Lucy bucked forward. "Please..." she begged.

Jake slid his tongue into her pussy, lapping at the feminine juices. His tongue slipped out again to grind against her clitoris before he inserted a finger again and began to ram her. He sucked forcefully on her clit waiting for her to come, knowing it would happen any second.

Lucy screamed when her body convulsed against his mouth. Her body arched, then she bucked wildly, shrieking incoherently with the force of her orgasm. She grabbed his hair and held his head tightly between her legs, nearly fainting with the intense tremors that shook her.

Even as the waves subsided, Jake lapped at her pussy. He couldn't get enough of the taste of her on his tongue. This night would be the only time her body would be his, and he wanted to remember everything. His licked and fingered her until her body began to move against his mouth once more, her head rolling from side to side as deep moans sounded from her throat.

Jake reared up and rammed his pulsing cock into her wet pussy, lifting her momentarily from the blanket. Lucy grunted, but matched his enthusiasm as she worked her hips, clenched her pussy lips tight, and rocked around him.

He latched onto a nipple with his lips as he pounded her vagina, amazed at her tightness and how nothing had ever felt better than having Lucy's hot body wrapped around his penis.

"Fuck me…fuck me in the ass…make me scream…" Her whispered plea set him on fire.

Jake flipped her roughly onto her stomach and dragged her ass up and over her bent knees.

"Fuck me…" Lucy arched her back and whipped her long hair across her shoulders.

He took his erection in his hand and clutched one smooth hip. Jake found her anus with the tip of his cock, but before he could slide into her, Lucy slammed against him and down his length. She was wild with excitement, wild with the moonlight glinting off her hair, and wild with passion just for him.

Jake pumped and ground into her ass, keeping up with the rhythm Lucy set. Heat began to build, and he knew there was nothing that could keep him from coming.

"I'm going to come in your tight ass!" he grunted with teeth clenched over the top of her back as his hips continued to thrust against her. Lucy slammed harder against him as her orgasm rolled through her lower body and streamed upwards to burn her breasts.

Jake growled and impaled himself inside her contracting body, holding her against him tightly as he came once more in waves.

Perspiration poured down his face, his heart thundered in his chest, and he knew without a doubt he would never have a sexual experience again that came close to matching this night with Lucy.

He withdrew his cock when her body fell forward to the blanket and dropped beside her, trying to catch his breath. Lucy lay motionless, her breathing as harsh and erratic as his. Finally, she rolled to her back and stared into the night sky. Her hand floated across the top of the blanket until she found his fingers. Clutching them tightly, he heard her whisper.

"I love you…only you, Matt. You'll never know how much…"

* * * * *

Her one statement rang in his ears as they dressed, kissed, and strolled back to the vehicle. It dogged him the miles he drove to her home. It reared up and pointed a finger of accusation when he slid the dress from her body in her bedroom and moaned with ecstasy as she straddled his body and rode him until they both came in waves once more.

Now, hours later, he stood looking at her curled beneath her quilt in the moonlight streaming through the window, her luxurious auburn hair spread across the pillow, and her mouth slightly open as she slept—and tried to forget how many times she had called him Matt.

His brother would never forgive him if he found out. A rueful smile curved Jake's mouth. *So what? I'll never forgive myself.* But he was helpless when it came to Lucy.

He shook his head, bent to tuck the blanket beneath her chin, and brushed his lips across her mouth, amazed that he was certain he'd fallen in love with her over the course of a few hours. *That shit is only supposed to happen in movies...*

Jake turned on his heel and strode from her bedroom. Lucy wouldn't be surprised when she woke. He'd said he couldn't stay until morning, but would be back as soon as he figured out a few problems at work. But it wouldn't be him coming back—it would be Matt, and Jake would never experience loving Lucy again.

* * * * *

Jake's cell phone rang. He rose from Matt's couch and raced across to his jacket, fumbling as he hurried to yank the phone out of the pocket. "Hello?"

"It's me." His brother's voice was edged with exhaustion.

Jake swallowed to keep his breathing even. "Hi, Matt. How'd everything go? Are you on your way back?"

"I'm about four hours out, tired as hell, but Steph is finally out of my life. Christ, what a ride down. She pleaded with me to take her back one minute, and screamed she hated me the next when I wouldn't give her any more money. She left Milwaukee with some sick joker who thinks she's the best thing that ever walked into his life."

"Do you think she's gone for good?"

"She damn well better be. I told her I'd put a restraining order out if she ever tried to contact me again."

The phone crackled between them, the only sound to break what Jake's guilt took to be uncomfortable silence.

"I don't know what I was thinking. I should have shoved the bitch on a bus and held my ground, but I was so upset that she'd find Lucy that I wasn't thinking straight."

More silence.

So, how did the reunion go? Did we pull it off? I feel like a real asshole doing that to Lucy, but she didn't need to hear about Steph."

Jake's stomach churned. "Good. She had a great time. You're going to have to learn how to jitterbug."

"You shit!"

Jake heard the relieved chuckle in Matt's voice.

"I hate to dance."

"Well, Lucy loves to. She thinks you're the cat's meow with your dancing expertise."

"How did things go afterwards? Did you get her to drink enough so she didn't ask you to stay the night?"

Jake rested his hand on the top of his head and glanced at the ceiling. "She never asked." It wasn't a lie. Lucy hadn't ask him to stay—he'd kept her mouth too busy kissing him all the way up the sidewalk and into the house. "Matt...you're a lucky guy. Lucy is a great gal. Boy, she sure loves you."

"I love her. I never want to have her find out about this. I swear it's the only time I'll ever lie to her."

"Well, there's no way you'd get me to do it again, buddy."

The phone crackled again.

"Jake?"

"I'm here."

"You okay?"

"Yeah, just tired. I didn't sleep too well last night. Maybe I'll take a nap since you'll be a while yet. I can drive all night and be back home in the morning."

"Why don't you stay a few days? I want you to 'formally' meet Lucy. She's asked once or twice when she gets to meet my brother. Besides, I'm having a few problems with subcontractors that you can help me out with."

"I don't think so."

"Come on, bro. I could really use your help."

Jake dropped to the surface of a chair and stared at his hands. "Seems to me I already helped you out." His chest ballooned with his deep sigh. Meeting Lucy as 'Jake' would have to happen sooner or later. "All right, Matt. I've got to go home for a day or so and take care of few things. Then I'll be back."

* * * * *

Matt hurried up Lucy's wet sidewalk. It was near midnight and raining, but he couldn't stand the thought of waiting to see her until the next day. Tomorrow was Sunday and there was no way he would spend one minute of it without her company.

He'd only spoken a few minutes to Lucy on the cell, telling her he'd been busy most of the day with some problem at work, thankful that Jake had given him an excuse to be gone so long. All he had managed to tell her was that he'd be at her place by midnight before her phone went dead due to a storm.

Matt's eyes took in the darkness of the yard. Apparently her power was still out from the earlier storm. He took the porch steps two at a time and, before he reached the door, it swung open. Lucy stood naked in the glow of the candles she'd lit about the room, her long hair curling around her breasts and a loving smile set on her lips.

She launched herself into his arms. "It's been a long night waiting for you," she whispered when he finished kissing her.

Matt's fingers lifted her hair to expose a breast, bent forward, and kissed the tip. "I would've driven faster if I'd have known you were naked and waiting for me."

"I'm always waiting for you." Lucy already had his shirt unbuttoned and worked on his zipper as he backed her into the house and through the kitchen doorway. Whenever he was in the same room as her, the same hot waves of desire washed over him time and time again.

Matt backed her up to the edge of the table, grasped her hips, and hiked her body to sit on the surface. His middle finger entered her pussy a second later, his thumb grinding against her moist clitoris. His lips left hers when he gently pushed her onto her back and used his free hands to drag her knees wider.

Her pussy lips glistened in the candlelight. Matt withdrew his finger, spread her labia wide, and licked her clitoris. He captured the bud with his lips and sucked greedily, smiling when her hips began to grind.

He dragged her closer to the edge and slid his cock into her waiting heat. "I've thought about this all day. I just can't get enough of you." He kept his strokes slow, teasing her as she wiggled around him.

"Matt…" Lucy grabbed his bare hips and urged him deeper inside of her. "Please, fuck me harder. I can't stand this!"

His strokes became more rapid as he slid in and out of her pussy, the frantic hammer of their fucking causing both to explode immediately.

Lucy pulled his mouth to hers as the sparks of her orgasm receded, smiling with satisfaction as she nuzzled his lips. "Wouldn't I have been surprised if you were someone from the electric company?"

He threw his head back, laughing as he pulled her upright to sit on the edge. "Yup! He would have gone back to his coworkers, told them about his house call, and you would have had a group of guys taking turns at cutting your power every night just to get inside the house."

She kissed him again. "I missed you today. It's been way too long since we made love." She sat back and smoothed her hand over his whiskered jaw. "Thank you for last night, Matt. I had a fabulous time."

Guilt poked at him, but he ignored the jab, yet wondered at the same time how Jake managed to get out of the house without making love to her the evening before. He pushed the thought aside, however. The ruse was over. "Say, how would you like to go on a picnic tomorrow? We'll pick up some food somewhere and go out to the lake."

"Ooo…and spend the day on a blanket with you?" Instantly, the image of him making wild love to her the night before made her heart skip a beat. She could still feel the heat of his cock sliding in and out of her rectum. "I don't know if that's a safe thing to do in broad daylight! I know how you can be."

"Well, hon," he kissed the tip of her nose, "if it gets to be too much for either of us, we'll just come back here."

Chapter Nine: Forever Isn't Without End

Jake drove down Colby's main street on Monday morning, searching for a place to stop for a cup of coffee, using that excuse as a way to build his courage before visiting Matt out at the construction site. He had never even returned to Milwaukee as planned. The continual guilt of making love to Lucy ate at him as each mile passed, causing Jake to finally slam on the brakes, turn the truck around, and head back to come clean with his brother. The two had never held secrets from one another and Jake was not about to start now. Somehow, Matt would forgive him—the twin brothers were too close for things to be any other way. And somehow, he would bury the burgeoning feelings of love for Lucy that he couldn't lay to rest. No woman had ever affected him the way she did, but he would have to forget the need she'd created inside of him from the first time he saw her standing on the other side of the screen door.

Jake eased his truck into a parking spot, grabbed his wallet from where it lay on the dash, and locked the door behind him as he got out. Stretching the kinks from his back, he waited for a car to pass by before walking across the street to a small café with the neon *OPEN* sign blinking in the window. As he entered the building, a tinkling was heard over his head.

An older couple just leaving their booth sent him a cursory glance as he crossed the tiled floor and sat at the counter. A moment later, he was the only patron in the place. He grabbed a menu, flipped it open, and tried to concentrate on the different choices before him as he pushed aside his rehearsed apology speech to Matt.

"Well, hello there, young man!"

He glanced up to see an elderly woman waddling through the swinging doors to the kitchen. A huge smile creased her face.

"Didn't expect to see you here this early."

Jake glanced quizzically around the diner to see whom she spoke to. He'd thought that he was the only customer. He was.

"Something wrong, Matt? You look puzzled as hell."

A grin curved his mouth when he realized the woman thought he was his brother. "You must be talking about my twin brother, Matt." He eyed her closely. "Say, don't I know you? You're not Mavis Johnson, are you?"

"Jake Diamond, is that you?"

He extended his arm to grasp her waiting hand. "At your service! Mavis, it's been years!"

"Eighteen to be exact! Why, the last time I saw you was when I called the ambulance because you fell out of that tree the day your family moved out of town!"

Jake chuckled as he perched back on the stool. "You remember that?"

"Honey, in this small town, a boy falling out of a tree is something to remember." She leaned forward with ponderous breasts resting on the empty tray she carried and studied him closely with a shake of her head. "It's absolutely amazing, Jake, how much you look like Matt. I could have sworn it was him sitting here when I came through those doors."

"So, you've met back up with Matt?"

She chuckled loudly. "Why, he's one of our regulars. Likes the 'menu' around here if you know what I mean." Her bushy eyebrows lifted when she enunciated the word menu.

"Hey, Mavis! I need your help back here!" The male voice came from the kitchen.

"That would be Pete, the cook. Helpless SOB if I ever saw one. Are you here to visit your brother?"

Jake nodded. "He's working at the old school. I can't believe that so many years have gone by. How have you been?" Except for the gray hair, Mavis hadn't changed a bit.

"I've been good. This place here keeps me young."

"Mavis!" The voice echoed again, this time with a peevish edge to it.

Mavis rolled her eyes. "I'd love to visit, but I better see what the hell's the problem back there. Were you going to order?"

"No, I think I'll just have a cup of coffee and a doughnut."

Mavis poured him a cup, scooped a doughnut from a glass container, and smiled widely when she set them both before him. "Well, son, I'd like to sit and BS with you a little longer, but duty calls." She nodded her head in the direction of the kitchen and disappeared a second later.

Jake made quick work of the bakery and coffee, and soon tired of waiting for Mavis to return to the front. Now that he was in town, his guilt urged him to find his brother before he lost his nerve. Fishing a five-dollar bill from his wallet, Jake tossed it onto the counter and headed for his truck.

The café door hadn't even slammed behind him when he ran smack dab into Lucy on the sidewalk. His jaw clenched in agitation just before she flung herself into his arms and molded her body to his.

"Matt! I didn't think I'd see you until tonight!"

Before Jake could say a word, Lucy pulled his mouths to hers and planted a kiss of promise against his lips.

Instant heat swirled in Jake's stomach and, without thought, he returned the enthusiastic embrace with one of his own.

Lucy finally broke the contact, grabbed Jake by the hand, and hauled him around the building to the alley in the back where she again molded her pubic mound against his erection. She kissed his neck, sucked on his earlobe, and slid a hand between them to knead the outline of his hard penis. "Why is it that I can't get enough of you?" she breathed out. "You make me hot, you make me wet. The only thing I can think of is your cock inside me."

Jake's stomach tumbled as he held her close, relishing the feel of her sweet body next to his. He had never planned to hold her in his arms again. *Just one more time…*

Lucy continued to stroke his jean-covered erection. "Can you slip away a little longer? I was going into the café to get something, but it can wait. Let's go to my house." Her green eyes glittered with anticipation at the thought of the stolen time — something she hadn't planned on. She'd awoken this morning, kissed him goodbye and planned to spend her day shopping after she picked up her paycheck.

Jake pulled her body closer so he wouldn't have to look into her eyes as he fought a huge battle to walk away, but knew that a white flag already waved in surrender. Lucy was just too much to resist. *It would only be this last time…Matt…I'm sorry…* "How about I meet you at your house? We'd have to leave right now so I can get back to work." It was just a small lie.

She stood on her tiptoes and kissed him once more. "Let's go. We'll take our own vehicles so you can get going as soon as possible." She took him by the hand and led him back to the front of the building. Stopping, she looked around the street, and then turned in surprise. "Where's your Suburban?"

Son of a bitch… "I…I used one of the guys' trucks. My vehicle was blocked in."

"Okay! Hurry — I can't wait to get naked in your arms."

Watching her scurry to her car, Jake jumped forward and grabbed her waist before she tripped headlong into the parking meter. "Whoa, Luce, you're going to hurt yourself one of these days."

Lucy didn't even blush anymore at her own clumsiness. Matt was used to it by now since her constant awkwardness was a daily occurrence.

Jake just shook his head with a smile. Some things never changed. He watched her yank her keys from somewhere deep inside her purse, toss him a smile of thanks over her shoulder, and enter the car just before she peeled out to head for home.

Jake was a half a block behind her the entire way. He skidded to a stop behind her car just as she slammed the driver's door and lit out for the porch.

He scrambled after her, leapt up on the porch, and chuckled when the front door slammed in his face as she raced into the house. Her giggle echoed through the screen, following by the sound of her running feet as she raced across the living room. By the time Jake followed the same path, she was already at the top of the stairs. He jumped over her cotton shirt where it lay on the bottom step, more excited by the minute when he realized she was undressing herself as she ran. Her lacy bra floated by his face and when he looked up, all he saw was her jean-clad ass and bare back as she disappeared from sight.

Jake yanked his t-shirt over his head, stumbled on the top step in his urgency to get his hands on her, and raced to her bedroom door.

Lucy was trying to kick off her jeans, her large breasts bouncing when the cuff of one leg refused to slide over a slim ankle. Her handicap allowed him the final steps before he snaked one arm out and dragged her to the bed.

They fell across the surface, their tongues darting between the lips of the other, giggling and chuckling as they quickly stripped off the rest of their clothes to feel the naked skin of the other. Their hilarity soon turned to moans of excitement as large hands rushed to cup full breasts and slender fingers curled around a throbbing cock.

"I'm so glad I ran into you," Lucy whispered as she stroked him.

Jake pulled her across his chest and massaged her ass. "Me too." He framed her face with his hands and stared up into her smoldering eyes. "I love you, Lucy." If felt so good to say it out loud—words from his heart, not a pretend declaration supposedly from his brother. The freedom to say the words audibly after they had pounded in his brain over the last few days was like a huge weight lifting off his shoulders. He would have this one last time with her and no one was going to stop him. "I don't think I've ever felt about a woman like I feel about you."

She dipped her head and kissed him softly. "You make feel so special. You make me feel like I can accomplish anything because you're by my side. I love you, too." Her tongue followed the line of his mouth, down under his square chin, and stopped to suckle the hard dart of his nipple. Lucy smiled from beneath her lashes and continued to lick a moist path over the wiry hair of his chest to his navel.

Jake's stomach muscles tightened as her mouth continued lower, knowing where her magnificent lips were going to stop.

Lucy continued to tease him with her tongue, coming close, but never quite taking his penis into her mouth until she repositioned her body, straddled his chest, and spread herself above his face, searching for his lips against her pussy. "Lick me," she whispered just before she drew her mouth over the tip of his penis and began to suck.

Jake spread her pussy lips open with his thumbs and starting at her clitoris, licked through the wet feminine slit that hovered above his mouth, and back again. Lucy trembled above him as she sucked his entire length with moans of excitement in the back of her throat.

Closing his eyes, Jake used his fingers to guide him. Sliding his index finger along her crack, he found her anus and inserted a finger, working it in and out of her body as she thrust against his hand with her ass. His tongue flicked her clitoris before gently latching on to the swollen bud with his teeth to entice her body closer to orgasm.

Shards of promising heat shot through Lucy's body as she sucked greedily at his cock with her mouth and stroked his hard length with one hand. Two fingers were jammed up her pussy before Jake lifted her off of him and forced her onto her stomach. Sliding over her, he used his knees to spread her legs wide and slid strong hands around the curve of her hips to rest between the smooth firmness of her belly and the mattress top. She felt the roughened heat of his hand searching lower until his fingers came in contact with her clitoris. Simultaneously, Jake's penis found her wet pussy hole and slid easily into the hot tight tunnel. Small grunts of pleasure echoed in her ear with each thrust against her spread body.

The instant effect of being flattened by his body weight with his hands working against her pussy and his long cock pounding against her cervix put Lucy over the edge. She couldn't thrust back like she wanted to. She couldn't push forward into his hand as she craved to do. She could only lie flat—completely at his mercy—and it caused huge waves of heat to ripple through her body. Her orgasm quivered around his cock, wracking her body time after time until they slowed along with her gasps of pleasure.

Lucy loved this Matt—the one who was rougher than usual with her—the one who would force her face down to accept whatever he felt like doing with her body. Only one other night—that was the evening of the reunion—had he made love to her with the edge of suppressed strength and complete dominance. He was the master who thrilled her body and sucked at her soul.

She didn't fight him when his palms slid around her waist to drag her upwards to her hands and knees. Lucy still trembled from the most recent orgasm and waited on the center of the bed with excitement to see what he would demand next. "Tell me what you want to do to me."

"I want to fuck you up the ass. But first..." Jake moved away from her and stood beside the bed, his penis standing straight up with the tip glistening. "Suck me again. I love your mouth around my cock. I want you to taste yourself." He placed his hands on his narrow hips and waited as she crawled closer. She reached out to hold him with one hand, but Jake grasped her firmly by the wrist. "No. Just with your mouth. That's all I want to feel around me."

Lucy hid her smile as she glanced up at him. "I'll only use my mouth if you promise not to move. You can't fuck me back — as soon as you do, you lose your chance to fuck me in the ass."

His dark gaze smoldered as he tightened the grip of his fingers on his hips, ready to meet her challenge, and waited silently.

Lucy opened her mouth and licked the dew from the end of his penis, enjoying the tiny jump of his sex organ. Swirling her tongue around the tip, she opened her mouth wider and slid it halfway down his shaft—and tasted her pussy on the velvety skin. Drawing back up to the tip, she began to nibble him gently in between long tortuous licks. It was all she could do to keep her palms flat on the bed. Her mouth clamped over him again, and Lucy began to suck mightily each time her lips found the base of his erection and worked their way to the tip. Her head began to bob. Opening her eyes, she spied his clenched fists at his side as he tried to remain still. The narrowing of his gaze told her that he knew exactly what she was up to. Lucy was going to drive him mad with her own demand.

She licked his cock down one side until she came to his balls nestled in dark pubic hair. Gently, Lucy kissed his scrotal sac, sporadically popping one testicle into her mouth before moving to the other, and then worked her way back up his shaft to dart her tongue into the small dripping slit at the end, loving the masculine smell and taste that was simply Matt.

Suddenly, his arms were around her again as he pushed her mouth from his cock, and he flipped her body around on the bed so her ass faced him. The pressure of one hand at the back of her head forced her down until her cheek lay against the bedspread, and her ass was spread before him. Jake yanked her body to the edge of the bed and plunged his cock into her pussy, stroking at a regular rhythm.

Lucy tried to raise up to all fours, but her head was forced back down against the bed. Her heart pounded with excitement before she tossed him another challenge. "I thought you were going to fuck me in the ass?" She thrust her pussy backwards against him and clenched tightly.

"I'm going to," he hissed between clenched teeth. "You're dripping. I'm getting my cock wet so I don't hurt you." He pulled out of her pussy, spread her ass cheeks with his hands and was inside her rectum a second later, pounding against the tightness.

Lucy grunted and slammed back against his cock, the heat building faster than it ever had before. She would never tire of him taking her this way. She would never come to the day that she didn't want him inside her. Matt rocked her world with the intensity of his fucking. Her fingers curled around a pillow as her orgasm rocketed through her clitoris, raced through her womb, and heated her breasts. Lucy screamed against the bed.

Jake jerked inside of her, grabbed her hips tightly and came, his semen leaking out around his penis as he continued to stroke. Goosebumps raised the skin on his arms as he gasped for air. "God, Lucy, I love you!"

But this will be the last time to ever enjoy your body...

Chapter Ten: The Ruse Is Up

Lucy returned to the café later that day to gather her paycheck, hoping that she would be able to make it to the bank before the window closed. She still glowed from the aftermath of the fierce lovemaking session with Matt. Every time she thought of how powerful he was, how he had manhandled her body with controlled strength, her heart raced and her stomach did a flip.

Taking another deep breath, she dropped her purse on the shelf behind the cash register and waved at Mavis when she popped her gray head over the swinging doors. "Just me, Mavis. I came to pick up my check."

The older woman smiled and walked behind the counter a moment later with a tray of clean glasses. "Are you going to the bank?"

"Mmmm-mmm," Lucy answered Mavis, giving more attention to the money sack where she knew she'd find her check.

"Would you drop off my check at the same time? Dana called and said she's having problems with a babysitter. I don't think she'll get to work in time for me to take care of any banking."

Lucy flipped through the various envelopes, finally spotted one with her name on it, and turned to lean casually against the counter. She stared dreamily into space with a permanent smile set on her lips.

Mavis crossed her arms beneath her breasts, stared, and then shook her head. "What do you look all happy for?"

"It's a beautiful day. I ran into Matt before lunch and…" her cheeks took on a slightly rosy hue, "…and we had an opportunity to sneak back to my house. God, I love that man." Lucy sighed with contentment.

"So what did you do with his brother when the two of you were having a little late morning delight?"

Lucy continued to smile even as Mavis' words finally threaded their way through her hazy brain. "What brother?" She walked behind the counter to help with the clean glasses.

"Matt's brother."

Lucy straightened and looked around before she settled her questioning gaze on her coworker. "Did I miss something here? I don't know what you're talking about."

"Hello, Puddin' Head!" Mavis peered closely at the younger woman. "Is anyone in there?"

"Mavis, I give. What do you mean?"

"Matt's brother, Jake. He was in here earlier. In fact, I saw you take him by the hand and lead him down the street." She saw the confusion in Lucy's eyes. "Where did you two go?"

"I didn't go anywhere with Matt's *brother*. In fact, I've never met him. If you're talking about late this morning, I was coming in to get my check, but I ran into Matt coming out the door and we went back to my house. He never said anything about his brother being in town."

Mavis' brow dipped into a frown—just before her mouth opened to let out one of the biggest laughs that Lucy had ever heard. The woman bent over the counter, pounding a beefy fist on the surface as she tried to control her hilarity. "Oh, my God! They did it again!" All six patrons that sat at the various tables turned in astonishment to stare at the hiccupping woman.

"Did what?" Lucy grabbed Mavis' arm and squeezed it tightly. "Mavis, what's going on that I don't know about?"

"The Diamond boys have struck again!" She wiped her wet cheeks with the corner of her apron. Her head nodded in the direction of stool at the end of the counter. "You had better sit down and think this through."

Lucy clamped her mouth shut and stalked behind the counter until she flopped onto a stool. Her brain raced, trying to figure out what her friend was trying to say. She had a sinking feeling that she wasn't going to like it, because already her brain refused to accept a certain possibility.

Mavis followed and took a seat beside her. "Lucy, Matt has a twin brother named Jake."

"I know he has a brother, but I didn't know they were twins."

"Those two boys were something else when they were younger. They pulled the old switcheroo more than once just for the fun of it. You see, no one could tell them apart. They looked alike then and are exactly the same now. Hell, Jake was in here this morning. I thought it was Matt until he corrected me. He said he was in town to visit his brother. Honey, you were talking to him outside."

Lucy's face paled before her eyes. Mavis thought the young woman was going to faint when her body went limp, and she nearly fell off the stool only to be saved by Mavis' girth. "Lucy! Lucy, girl! What's wrong?"

Lucy's world spun as she clung to the elderly woman's arm. Her watery gaze looked up into the now concerned face swimming above her. "I have to get out of here..." she whispered.

"You're not going anywhere the way you are. Honey, you're scaring me."

Three customers at a table behind them stared closely to figure out what was going on. Lucy barely noticed their looks of concern as she staggered from the stool with tears on her cheek. Mavis grabbed her hand, supported her waist with one arm, and led her through the kitchen past a wondering Pete and out into the alley. She pointed a finger at the obviously upset Lucy. "Stay here. I'm going to grab a chair." Thirty seconds later, she pulled a metal seat through the door and forced the younger woman onto it. "Now, take a breath and tell me what happened."

Lucy's face dropped into her upturned palms. She trembled and gulped to gather more air into her lungs. It wasn't long before tears streamed over her fingers and down her cheeks.

Mavis forcibly shook her shoulders. Not receiving any response, she rested her arm around Lucy's heaving shoulders. "It's okay, honey, you just cry. When you're done, you can tell me and then we'll figure out a solution."

"I'll kill him..." The muffled words were choked out between sobs.

"Kill who?"

"Who she gonna kill?" Pete opened the back door and stared at the disheveled Lucy. "Maybe she can do it when you're not working, Mavis. We gotta new customer."

Mavis shot up from where she was bent over the weeping woman, balled her fist, and shook it menacingly into the air. "Pete, I'm gonna rap you in the nuts if you don't get the hell out of here! Take care of the goddamned customer yourself!" Before she had a chance to take a step in the man's direction, Pete jumped backwards and slammed the inside door. She turned back to Lucy. "Now, take a deep breath and let me have it."

One of Lucy's hands dropped limply to her thigh as she used the back of other hand to swipe the tears from her cheeks.

"Who you going to kill, Lucy?"

"Matt, that's who. And maybe his brother — if I can find two bullets." The last weeks of thinking she was crazy in love crashed inside her brain. She was such a fool.

"Honey, it was probably just a little joke they played on you. Come on, you know Matt loves you. That man is crazy about you!"

Lucy looked up, pain turning to anger in her fiery eyes. "You don't understand. I'll never forgive him."

Mavis hated to see her this way. This summer was the happiest she had ever seen Lucy. "Go talk to him. Have him explain."

"I *said* you don't understand. How can he explain why he allowed his brother to have sex with me?"

Mavis' head snapped back, her eyes bulged, and her mouth flopped open. "*Sex?* What the hell are you talking about?"

"Today! Today I thought I was having sex with Matt! *Today!* But you're telling me it was his brother!" Lucy grabbed the arm of the other woman. "Mavis, are you sure? Are you sure it was Jake who I ran into today. Because if it was, he never had a chance to switch places with Matt if what you're telling me is true. He never left my sight all the way home and all the way up into my bedroom where he banged the hell out of me." The tears started again. "He made crazy, hot love to me, Mavis—he even said he loved me for chrissakes!" Her voice rose as she continued to put it all together in her head. "OH, my God! It was Jake with me at my reunion!"

"Now, don't start thinking the worst. Jake insinuated that this was the first time he was back in town after all these years."

Lucy's head shook. "I don't know how they did it, but I tell you, it was Jake who went to the reunion with me. It was Jake who danced with me all night. Matt would rather just sit and talk. And it was Jake who made love to me that night also!" Her lids fluttered shut as she thought about the way she made love earlier with the man she thought was Matt. The brother who had sex with her on Friday night possessed the same powerful strength that she was mooning about only fifteen minutes ago. They may look alike, but they were different in bed. Only now, after she knew about their deceit, was she able to separate them in her mind.

Suddenly, she grabbed Mavis' arm again. "And one of them has a scar!" Her gaze darted about as she once again aligned the facts together in her mind. "That would be Jake! I hadn't noticed that scar until last Friday night." She squeezed her eyes shut and thought long and hard, picturing the powerful, naked man she was with earlier that day. It was easy to remember the scar above his nipple as she looked up while giving him a blowjob. She had seen it again. The only other time was when they were parked in the Suburban at the stream after the party.

Lucy felt Matt's betrayal deep into her heart. Pulling off this sham was the worst thing anyone had ever done to her. He had taken her all-consuming love and squashed it into the ground with his stupid boyish prank. He was like all the others.

She stood and brushed off the back of her jeans, her jaw tight with anger. Mavis took one look and knew there would be trouble.

"Listen, Luce. There's got to be some kind of explanation..." Her words tapered off unconvincingly.

"You bet there's going to be an explanation. I can't wait to hear why they thought it would be great sport to stomp on my feelings! How could they have done it, Mavis? Well, I'll tell you what. They're going to explain it to me—just before I walk out of both of their lives!" She rounded the woman, yanked the back door open, and stalked through the kitchen. Peter turned to glare at her. "What the hell are you looking at?" Lucy spouted across the kitchen as she strode by.

Pete turned quickly and continued to wash the pot in his hands.

* * * * *

Lucy sat on her porch with Mr. Pibbs cuddled in her arms. She had cried until she couldn't imagine that she would ever shed another tear. Then she got so angry that she screamed until the cat scuttled away to hide. When she started crying again, he came back to find comfort in her lap.

Scratching him now behind his ears in apology, she stared absently down the road, wondering if she would ever be happy again. "Men are bastards."

The cat meowed lightly and began to purr.

"I'm going to confront them. No, I'm not. I'm going to set them up. Let the two of them fuck each other." Her mind swam with different ideas, each more outlandish than the next. "You know what I'll do, Pibbs? I'll tie them down, cut off their balls and have buck-toothed Pete deep-fry them. Then I'll shove them up their ass. That's what I'll do. You know what? Maybe I won't cut off their nuts right away. First, I think I'll have the time of my life fucking both of them. Then let them go back and compare stories. Sooner or later, they'll be at each other's throats. When they come crawling to me with the truth, I'll turn and walk away. That's what I'll do, and I won't trip either!"

With determination squaring her jaw, Lucy rose from the swing to go back into the house and call Matt. He had promised her dinner at Angelo's. She would begin to call in her markers tonight.

Chapter Eleven: The Confession

Jake pulled his vehicle up to the construction trailer. His fingers nervously tapped the steering wheel as he stared at the entry door. His gaze wandered around the site and settled on Matt's Suburban parked off to the side.

Shit! There goes my one chance to not have to explain this today...

Sheer determination was the only thing that moved his hand to the ignition. A quick flick of the wrist and the motor quit humming. Jake breathed deeply three times to clear his head, opened the door, and walked up the steps of the trailer only seconds later. Before he had a chance to cross the small deck, the metal door opened. Matt smiled out at him.

"Jake! I didn't expect you until the middle of the week! Come on in and sit yourself down." He glanced at his watch. "You know, I've been here since six this morning. Give me ten minutes and we'll head on over to my apartment. You showing up works out great. I planned to take Lucy to Angelo's tonight. I insist you come along to meet her. Well, you've already met her, but Lucy doesn't know you yet." He clapped his hands and rubbed his palms together. "Hell, I can't wait for the two most important people in my life to get to know each other the way you two should."

Jake was rattled. Should he tell Matt here or wait until they went back to his apartment? *If I wait, I'll lose my nerve.* "Matt, can we talk about something?"

"Sure thing." Matt walked behind his desk. "Can you talk while I put some papers together?"

Jake shrugged and found it hard to meet his brother's eyes.

A shiver ran up Matt's spine. Since they were small children, one could always sense the other's emotions. Jake was terribly upset about something. He sat down slowly, never taking his eyes from his brother's face. "This isn't good, is it, Jake? What's going on?"

A wistful smile curved Jake's mouth as he settled on the couch, rested his elbows across his knees and clamped his hands together. "We haven't done this for awhile."

"Done what?"

Jake shrugged again. "You know. One minute you were inviting me in, excited that I was here. The next? " He looked across the room. "You knew that something was wrong. We have that special connection that most brothers don't have."

"Most brothers aren't lucky enough to be a half of a whole. That's what we are, Jake. We're twins. We spent every moment of our lives together until the last five years when this damn business has separated us. Some might think that's strange. I don't. You're my other half and that's just the way of it. I apologize for not realizing something was wrong the minute you walked out of that truck."

Jake smiled sadly at the floor. "Listening to you talk, you'd think you were the older brother. I got you by ten minutes, you know."

"Yes you do. Now, are you going to tell me what's wrong? We can figure it out whatever it is. Do you need money? What's mine is yours."

Jake's head snapped up. Matt had just given him the perfect opportunity to drop his bomb. He cleared his throat and hoped that this moment wouldn't be the last time his brother would have complete trust and love in his gaze. "Matt?" He cleared his throat one more time. "You just said "what's mine is yours". Does that include Lucy?"

Matt's body stiffened. "That's a stupid question."

Jake rose, crossed to the window, and stared out into the late afternoon sun. "Not so stupid if I tell you that I'm in love with her."

"What the hell happened last Friday? You never said anything." Matt's heart pounded against his ribs.

Jake turned to face him. "Before we go any further, I want you to tell me something. How quickly did you fall in love with her? Everything we do, Matt, we do alike. I'm willing to bet you fell for her the first day—just like I did. Don't look at me like that. I'm just trying to put things in order. Why would loving a great woman be any different from anything else we've ever done?"

Matt leaned forward in the chair, never taking his eyes from the man across from him. "Simply for the sake of 'putting things in order', I did fall for her the first night. I'll admit my initial thoughts were to get between her legs. It had been awhile since Stephanie, and I took one look at Lucy's breasts and figured they would be great to have in my hands. We went to dinner. By the end of the meal she had me hooked with her sweetness and her complete faith in the human race. Lucy might bumble her way through her days at times, but she's the soul mate I never thought I would find." He leaned back in the chair and fought his churning stomach. "Now, what happened last Friday?" He watched his brother's response to his question. Jake ran a trembling hand through his thick hair. Matt instantly knew what was going to come out of his mouth.

"We had sex."

"You son of a bitch." Matt bolted from his chair.

Jake pointed a finger. "You stay right there. And don't be calling me a son of a bitch. I've done enough of that myself over the last day and a half."

The silence bounced off the walls. Matt's chest heaved in an attempt to control his anger, and then he sat stiffly in the chair once more. His muscled jaw silently quivered.

"I tried, Matt, to do it your way—and it backfired. I did what you asked. I covered for you so you could get rid of that bitch, Steph, and not involve Lucy. I gave her the night of her life. She was a hit, and I played it to the hilt until I realized I wasn't playing anymore. I wanted to please her. I wanted to hold her in my arms on the dance floor. Do you know how hard it was to keep my hands off her when she constantly rubbed up against me?"

Instant jealously pierced Matt's heart. How in hell did he ever think that his hot-blooded Lucy would simply hold hands with his brother, when normally she had her hands in his pants trying to get a hold of his hard-on? He brought his silent attention back to Jake's confession.

"I got her drunk like you said to, but not drunk enough."

"Apparently not."

"Christ, Matt. She had enough to drink that she should have been flat on her ass. She wouldn't keep her hands off me. She kept thanking me for the wonderful night and wouldn't take no for an answer. I tried to push her away, but nothing worked."

"You could have done something." Matt's flat voice was filled with accusation.

Jake spread his arms wide. "Do you want to hear everything? Because if you do, you better be ready to accept the actions of the little fireball you created over the past weeks. I was supposed to be you, remember? You asked me to do this for *you*. In fact, I remember that you wouldn't take no for an answer. So, do you want to hear it all?"

Matt nodded his head in silent approval for Jake to continue, knowing that the consequences of making the switch were finally stacking up on his shoulders.

"She wouldn't leave me alone. I almost swerved off the road more than once because she was practically sitting in my lap, begging me to make love to her—and telling me the things she wanted to do to me."

Matt's eyes closed momentarily, then quickly snapped open to rid himself of the vision Jake's words created in his mind. He understood perfectly well how persuasive Lucy could be. He swallowed back the hurt, his brother's betrayal, and his own disloyalty to their brotherhood by asking Jake to do something that would harm the perfect connection they'd always had. "Where did it happen?" He crossed his fingers like a young boy would, hoping that it had not been in the same bed he's made love to her in so many times.

Jake decided to forego the fact that she had given him one of the greatest blowjobs of his life in the Suburban before they even got out of the vehicle. "We stopped on a side road by a stream and got out of the vehicle. She insisted on taking the blanket from your backseat and spreading it in the grass." Both hands now traveled through his thick hair. "If it's any consolation, she continually said she loved you. You, Matt. Not me. It was your name on her lips. It was our deceit that we ever put her in that position in the first place."

Matt's jaw continued to clench as he kept a tight check on his emotions. "Was that the only time?" He watched his brother's face closely. Guilt flashed in the eyes that mirrored his own. "Well, you just answered my question. Where? When?"

Jake's chin hung to his chest. "I'm sorry, Matt. I went into the house with her. There was no stopping either of us. When I left in the middle of the night, I knew how I felt about her. And I was going to walk away and never touch her again."

Just the cadence of his voice made Matt's heart tumble again. "But you did. When? When could you have had a chance? You left for home. Oh, shit. Don't tell me you were with her today." Matt's fist pounded the desk. "What the fuck were you doing with her today?" Anger blazed anew in his eyes.

"I stopped at a café to get a cup of coffee before coming out here to confess."

"Lucy had the day off," Matt ground out.

"Yeah. I was leaving and ran into her right out in front as she was coming in to pick something up. She screamed your name and jumped into my arms. Before I knew it, she was begging for me to come to the house before going back to work. I'm sorry, Matt, but I couldn't stop myself. I didn't *want* to stop myself. I wanted one more time with her as the man she loved, because that's how I felt about her."

Matt stood, silently shuffled papers into an open drawer, and lifted out his keys. "I'm going to dinner with Lucy. You're not invited. I've got to think this through, Jake. I never would have thought you would do this to me."

"Come on, Matt. Please don't let this come between us. It's something we both cooked up. I'm not the only guilty party here. I wanted you to know so there would be nothing between us."

Matt wasn't in the frame of mind to give his brother's words any credibility at the moment. "You'll have to get a hotel room if you want to hang around. I can't think about this now and don't need to be tripping over you in my apartment. In fact, I don't know if I want to see you the rest of the week."

"Now look at who's being the bastard! Well, you can get hold of me when you're damn good and ready. I said my piece and that's it." Jake's finger pointed at his brother's chest once more. "Just remember whose idea this was in the first place — you goddamned well better remember that you begged me to step into your shoes. What the hell did you expect when Lucy's the hot little number that she is. And you had better not blame her for this or you can answer to me! I only wish I had someone like her!"

Matt relented slightly. As pissed as he was, he reached into his pocket and pulled out a key. He tossed it across the room and watched Jake's hand snatch it from the air. "I've changed my mind. Go back to my apartment. When I'm damn good and ready, you and I are going to discuss this again, and I don't want to be looking for you."

Jake spun, slammed the screen door against the wall, and left it swinging open as he hurried to his truck and peeled onto the highway thirty seconds later. Guilt coupled with anger ate at his insides.

Chapter Twelve: Let the Games Begin

Lucy's heart skipped a beat when Matt pulled into her driveway. At least she thought it was Matt. She'd have to figure it out before she initiated her plan. If it was really Matt here to pick her up, she would drive him crazy tonight with talk about the reunion and all the sex afterwards.

Greeting him at the door, Lucy swallowed her anger, flung herself into his waiting arms, and let the past feelings of love carry her through the first passionate kiss. No matter how pissed she was, Matt — or Jake — had a way of turning her to mush with simply a mere glance.

"I missed you today after you left." She ran her fingers lovingly across his jaw, watching his eyes closely for any response. Whoever held her in his arms was damn good at not showing his surprise or lack thereof.

"You haven't left my mind all day, Lucy. In fact, if we didn't have reservations, I'd haul you up those stairs right now and show you exactly what I want to eat for an appetizer."

Lucy battled her shiver of desire. It would be one way to find out who stood with her now. She would have a chance to see his chest and either the presence or absence of the tiny puckered scar. She wasn't ready to have sex with him, however. Instantly, an idea popped in her head. She'd know before they got to the restaurant.

"Well, you hold that thought and we'll discuss dessert back here when you're done wining and dining me!"

She brushed his erection with her hand and melted out of his arms, grabbed his hand, and led him through the open doorway.

Matt draped his arm across her slim shoulders and pushed the thought of Lucy stroking his brother's penis from his mind. Once they got to the passenger side of the truck, he scooped her into his arms, loving the sound of her giggle as he set her on the seat. He leaned forward, devoured the bodice of her low-cut sweater with his gaze, and rubbed his knuckles across the tops of her exposed breasts.

Her skin burned beneath his gentle touch.

"You sure you don't want to go back upstairs?" His gaze was hopeful.

Lucy shook her head, which caused light curls to sway across her shoulders. "Feed me, Matt. I need strength for the coming night."

"You are an absolute tease."

Lucy simply smiled. *You haven't even seen me in action yet, Mr. Diamond Whoever-You-Are.*

Once they were on the road, she unbuckled her seatbelt and slid across the seat, only to re-buckle herself in the middle.

Matt smiled and wrapped his right arm around her shoulders, then started slightly when her fingers caressed his crotch.

Lucy smiled up again. "I can't wait to play with this tonight. I'll have to order you something that has natural aphrodisiacs in it."

"Hah," he chuckled, "when I'm around you, I don't need anything to get me going. Just the sight of your naked body is enough."

Lucy laid her head on his shoulder as her hand traveled over his firm belly and across his chest. "Mmmm...I love you, Matt. Only you. I can't imagine my life without you in it." She played with the top button of his shirt, loosened it, and then moved to the next one. Her hand slid into his shirt to caress his right breast.

"You keep that up and we'll have to pull over. I love when you touch me." He could never get enough of her.

Lucy's hand swept across his breast twice, finding the skin absent of any scar, which confirmed that she was with Matt and not Jake. It amazed her that she couldn't tell the difference between the two brothers. She hid the wicked smile that curved her mouth upward. "If you want to stop, lets go to the same place where we made love after the reunion." He stiffened imperceptibly as soon as the words left her mouth. *Aha! Fire one!* "Although, it's still pretty light out and someone might see us. Remember how beautiful the moon was that night?" She leaned forward and looked up at the darkening sky through the windshield. "You know, we just might be lucky enough to have almost the same kind of night."

Settling back into the crook of his arm, Lucy sighed her contentment. "You're awful quiet. Is something wrong?"

"No," came his quick reply—almost too quick. "I'm just enjoying having you next to me."

"Let's do something special after we're done eating. Let's go to the same spot we did the other night. We'll take the blanket out again and go down by the stream."

Matt nearly cut off her words, but a morbid sense of curiosity kept his mouth shut. He wanted to know what had happened between Lucy and Jake.

When he remained silent, Lucy kept going. "I loved the feeling of you fucking me in the ass that night. It was better than usual."

It was all Matt could do to hold back the hiss that threatened to escape.

"You were so forceful. I couldn't believe when you flipped me over after eating my pussy for so long, and then jammed your cock into my ass. I don't know if it was the booze that made me come so many times that night or if it was your expertise, but wow, were you ever good." Lucy turned to nuzzle his neck and spied the angry tick in his cheek. *Fire two! My revenge has commenced!*

* * * * *

Lucy shoved her barely touched food aside as she reached forward for her unfinished glass of wine. The same wicked smile was back in place now, and she didn't give a damn if he wondered about it or not. Peeking beneath her lashes, she watched Matt count out numerous twenties and place them on top of the bill. She'd done her best to hit his pocketbook tonight. Instead of the usual inexpensive plate of spaghetti, tonight she'd ordered a side of lobster, three separate appetizers that were outrageously priced, and then begged for the most expensive bottle of wine on the menu. Matt had never said a word, but he'd looked confused at the sudden change of cuisine that she had merely pushed around her plate with her fork.

They sat huddled in a dark, romantic corner that had become their 'spot' whenever they visited Angelo's. Lucy leaned forward, grabbed Matt by his tie, and pulled his lips close. Her other hand found his crotch and she feather-stroked the burgeoning area with the promise of things to come.

Matt glanced around to see if anyone saw what was going on just beneath the table. Lucy would have to stop her playing if he was to be able to stand up without drawing attention to his erection. His large hand cupped her palm as he gently dragged her seeking hand back to the surface of the table. "Lucy, we'll never get out of here if you don't leave me alone. What's with you tonight? You've kept me in a constant state of arousal since we arrived. Not that I'm complaining—I love that you want me so bad."

She fanned her cheeks with the wine menu and giggled. "I think this wine is going to my head! I hope I can stay awake long enough to have some great sex tonight!" she tipped her chin and gazed up at him with a slight bat of her eyelashes. "Do you think you could top this morning?"

The flash in his eyes momentarily showed his confusion. Suddenly, his gaze narrowed.

Aha! Now he knows what I'm talking about – well, not really – it was Jake making crazy love to me earlier…Fire three!

"And just what did you like in particular this morning?" He struggled to keep the smile on his lips.

She grazed his bottom lip with the tip of her finger and smiled. "Oh, let's see. Hmmm…I guess all of it." She was going to make him beg for the details.

Matt imprisoned her wrist and pulled her finger away from his mouth as he stared down. His tongue wet his bottom lip in agitation. "Tell me exactly."

Her eyes glanced at her captured wrist first before she slowly glanced up again. "Oh, do you want to be rough again? I loved it when you were that way."

He simply remained closemouthed, waiting for her answer.

"Let's see," she pondered, "I loved how you chased me up the stairs. How cool was it that we were both naked by the time we got to the bedroom?" She watched his Adam's apple bob in his throat when he swallowed as she leaned forward and pressed her breasts against his upper arm. "I think this morning was the best sixty-nine session we ever had." She shook her head slowly with a smile. "The things you can do with your fingers. What I liked best, however, was how you pinned me to the mattress so I couldn't move, played with my pussy from the front and fucked me from behind. No, wait! Dragging my ass up was even better. I think this morning was some of the best anal sex ever." She thought his eyes were going to pop out of his head. Suppressed anger darkened his gaze further. "You were simply superb!"

"Let's get out of here." Matt grabbed her elbow and literally pulled her from the secluded booth, across the floor, and out the door. *I'll kill Jake for putting me through this.* Matt's gentler side, however, argued back. *You're just as guilty. You were the one who tried to pull one over Lucy's head. She didn't do anything that she normally wouldn't do.* He slowed his step, ashamed that he had manhandled her all the way to the car. For some reason, though, she didn't seem to mind. She just turned to face him with that sweet smile on her lips. Not being able to resist, he tipped his head and captured her mouth, tasting the expensive wine on her tongue. When they were finished, his hands gently cupped her face as he stared down. "I love you, Lucy. Sorry about being so rough. You drive me crazy with your talk. All I could think about was getting you out of the building and into my arms."

Warning bells went off in her head. As upset as she was with him didn't discount the fact that she still loved him. Or was it only him? What about Jake? Feelings of love raged this morning as he took her body and made her come time after time. Even she realized that her plan could turn sour as she tried to separate the two and bring revenge on both their heads.

She blinked, and then swallowed convulsively. The fact was, Lucy wanted Matt inside her. The man had a way of playing her body like the strings of a fine violin. So...why should she bite off her nose to spite her face? Lucy wanted to be fucked. "Let's go," she whispered. "I need you, Matt...I need you to make love to me." *Because it might be the last time...*

✳ ✳ ✳ ✳ ✳

Lucy stood in her room and ran her hand across Matt's naked chest, loving the feel of his firm muscles. Earlier, when he had offered to find a secluded spot on the way home, she declined, explaining to him that she wanted to continue to her house. The entire way, she had stroked his penis, teasing him until a dampened area around his zipper appeared. He was more ready for her than she could imagine.

Matt scalded her with his eyes as his hands gently brushed the contours of her toned body. "You're so beautiful..." His mouth dipped to capture a puckered nipple. His tongue circled the dart with slow, sensual licks that caused a moan somewhere deep in the back of her throat.

Earlier on the drive to her house, he had planned to take her roughly, ready to make her forget the times she was with his brother—ready to have no other experience compare to the times Jake had had sex with her. But that wasn't Matt's way. He would make slow, hot, and wet love to her until she screamed with pleasure. His fingers, his mouth, and his penis would drive her insane.

He scooped her into his arms, kissed her mouth, and laid her gently on the bed. A second later, his hand lightly touched her breasts and slid slowly down the soft curve of her hip, between her legs, and back to the smooth line of her jaw. Lucy arched against him, but he had other plans. "I'll be right back."

Her eyes snapped open in confusion. "Where are you going?"

He smiled and kissed the tip of her nose. "You just stay here. I'll only be a minute." Matt walked to her closet and disappeared inside. It wasn't long before he returned with scarves, his cloth belt, and a soft tie from one of her dresses.

Lucy rose to her elbows and stared. "What are you doing?"

"Care to play along with a little fantasy of mine?"

Her heart pounded as she was immediately drawn to the idea of something different. "Like what?"

"Lie back."

She did.

Matt lifted her arm and bound her wrist with a scarf. She watched as he secured it to the left side of the headboard. He copied his actions with her right arm. "Are you comfortable?"

Lucy nodded her head and fought to keep her breathing even. She wiggled her hands, but couldn't free them.

"Good. Now for your ankles." He looped his belt around her ankle and tied it to one of the posts at the foot of the bed. Grabbing up the tie from her dress, he pulled her legs wide and secured her other foot. He gazed at her pussy glistening in the candlelight. "I'm going to make you come time after time tonight. I'm going to play with your body until you can't take it anymore, then I'm going to make you come again."

Lucy's chest swelled with her excitement. Matt had never tried this before. Her anger was forgotten as she watched him crawl up onto the bed and between her splayed legs. She was at his mercy.

Matt began his assault. His hands slid leisurely up her calves, over her knees and up the inside of her thighs. His fingers rustled through the soft pubic hair that surrounded her pussy, then traveled a burning path to her breasts, ignoring the fact that she arched her mound against his hand, signaling that she wanted his fingers inside her. He loved the idea that he could do anything he wanted to and she wouldn't be able to escape. Lucy would be crazed with desire; exhausted from the many orgasms he had planned for her. This night would be burned into her brain.

Her heart beat out a rapid rhythm beneath his fingers when he took a breast in each hand, squeezed the generous mounds together, and then tweaked her hard nipples.

"Matt…" she breathed out in a near whisper.

He bent forward and leisurely kissed her. When Lucy darted her tongue between his lips, he pulled back. "I'm going to love driving you crazy." His hand traveled back between her legs as he stared into her eyes. Lucy's mouth gaped open when he ran a finger through her wet slit, refusing to enter her hot cave until he had her wiggling against her restraints. His finger flicked her clit, worked its way back between her labia to be moistened, and then returned to torture her throbbing bud.

"Please, Matt…"

"Uh-uh," his eyes twinkled with glee at her predicament. "Just let me play with you for a while." He reached for another scarf lying on the floor and blindfolded her.

Everything went dark. "Come on, Matt. I want to see you."

The mattress dipped beside her as his finger ran a damp path up and over her flat stomach. "Nope," his voice murmured beside her ear. "Tonight I want you tuned to the sensation of touch." Lucy's body jerked when teeth nipped at her nipple before the round bud was sucked into the moist cavity of his mouth.

Lucy's mind jumped from the sensation of his warm tongue at her nipple to follow his one wayward finger as it circled the curve of her opposite breast, trailed back to dip into her navel, and then haltingly floated downward until it swirled through her pubic hair again. The sexual tension in her body had her near to gasping. Her vaginal muscles clenched with the need to wrap tightly around his absent finger, his penis...it didn't matter, she simply needed something inside her. Lucy's body arched in response to the tickling sensation of his finger playing around her clitoris, but shivered when she realized he wasn't going to stroke it. Lucy arched against his hand, but her bound feet stopped any further movement to capture his teasing finger with her pussy. Lucy's hands curled around the sashes that secured her arms to the bedposts. Her spread-eagled position was comfortable, but her limbs were pulled wide and the ties were unforgiving. She ached to be fucked.

Matt's cock throbbed with the intensity of this sexual session. Having Lucy completely at his mercy excited him like no other time. It would be a night for her to remember always. Deciding to move things forward, he slid his body over hers, rested his weight on his elbows, pressed his erect cock against her pubic mound, and nibbled at her neck. Lucy bucked beneath him, her body searching for his penis, but he wouldn't give her what she desired so badly.

Hot breath heated her neck, and then the wetness of his tongue dampened the inside her ear while murmured words of love echoed around her.

He shifted above her body and reached down with a hand between them.

Lucy's heart pounded as she followed the motion in her head. Maybe now he would stick his cock inside her. Instead, the round head of his penis rippled through her moist folds, still not entering her heat.

Lucy squirmed and arched her hips when the pressure of his erotic glide left her. The heat continued to build in her lower body. The wetness from her pussy dripped a path to the bedspread she lay on. Hot sparks in her groin intensified when the full, hard length of his cock pressed against her mound once more.

"Matt...please...I'm going to come..."

Instantly, the tip of his cock circled her throbbing clit. Lucy groaned into the darkness that surrounded her. She arched her back, and came in wave after wave. The shards of her orgasm exploded through her belly, heating her breasts as masculine lips suckled one nipple and then the other. She bucked and gasped for air as the intense feeling suffocated her, searching for something to fill her. The orgasm wreaked havoc on her empty body, her pussy juices streamed out of her, but still, he would not penetrate her.

She lay gasping in the aftermath. Lucy's brain spun, her vagina clenched, and goosebumps covered the skin on her arms and legs.

The hot lips left her breasts. She waited breathlessly and was rewarded when his tongue returned to lick her midriff. She again followed its path in her mind as his body slid lower. Warm, moist darts swirled inside her navel, and then wet the inside of one thigh. Lucy gasped for air, her body immediately reacting to the idea that his mouth was close to her pussy.

She stared into the darkness of the blindfold. Gentle fingers spread her labia. She waited breathlessly to see what would happen next. Her body jerked as his tongue lapped its way through her wet slit. Blood rushed to her swollen clit when it was captured between warm lips. She bucked forward again; the instant heat of another orgasm building to crescendo. Her body rolled against the restraints as she worked her clit against the flicking tongue.

The overhead fan pressed cool air against her pussy as her lips were parted wider; the breezy chill was quickly replaced by the heat of his tongue darting into her hot tunnel, then was replaced once more with teasing licks. A thick finger filled her. She gasped. Moist lips returned to her clit and ground against it as he fucked her with his finger.

Lucy rocked her body, squeezing her muscles around his finger to hold them inside her.

The hot lips against her and the grinding finger produced another orgasm. It burst through her body as his finger jammed back and forth and his tongue wrapped around her bud.

She screamed this time, arching her back as she fought the restraints, but the heady assault continued. Her body trembled around three fingers now, the sucking sound of her wet pussy making her gasp for air once more. The onslaught didn't stop.

Matt lapped and sucked and alternated his tongue and his fingers time and time again until he coaxed her through another orgasm, and then waited for the vaginal spasms to slow. When her body lay still, his mouth and fingers disappeared only to be replaced with the heat of his body as he slid upwards to capture her mouth.

Lucy whimpered against his lips, opened her mouth, and their tongues danced against one another.

"God, I love you…" Matt whispered against her darting tongue. "I want to come inside you, but not yet…"

"Matt? Where…where are you? I can't take this any longer…"

The mattress dipped beside her and suddenly he straddled her chest. The weight of his penis rested between her breasts, then was gone a second later. Something hard bumped against her lips. Lucy latched on to his cock before it disappeared and sucked forcefully until his hips moved to the tempo she set. Her tongue whipped against his shaft, darting around his tip, and then his cock was gone again.

Matt spun away, his shoulders rising and falling as he inhaled air to stall his orgasm. Gaining control, he rolled back between her legs and dragged a pillow with him.

"Lift up your ass." His voice floated past her ears.

"No...I can't..." She raised her hips. A second later, she settled back into the softness beneath her, her lower body jutting upward as she was draped across the fluffy pillow. Her head lolled sideways as she waited. "I can't take this anymore...I want to hold you in my arms. Matt? Where are you?"

The heat of his breath preceded the gentle lick through her slit. "Are you uncomfortable?" he mumbled against her.

"God, no! My body feels like a quivering mass."

"You're not quivering now, Lucy, but you will be soon."

In her mind, she imagined the smile she knew accompanied his declaration.

Her breasts swelled with excitement. The pressure of one single finger was back. A warm tongue licked her again. She shivered when his fingers spread her folds again. A finger slid inside her. Something flicked against her clit just before his finger left her wet heat and traced a path down through the line of her slit. It stopped at her anus.

Lucy trembled and bit her lip to stop a sob from escaping. The tip of his finger circled her anus, teasing, until her legs strained against the bindings. She yearned to draw her knees to her chest to allow him better access. Soon, the pressure increased. Her rectum spasmed when one lone finger worked its way into her.

Lucy grunted, and then gasped when something filled her pussy. His cock! No! It was two fingers! Matt started his magic all over again. The pressure of being totally filled by him had her thrusting upward.

"That's it, baby. Does this feel good?"

"Yes! Oh, God, yes!" She clenched her muscles and rocked. "Harder! I need you to do it harder!"

His finger immediately slid further into her ass and the pressure nearly drove her to the edge of insanity.

Something else now circled her clit. Lucy was in such a state that she couldn't tell any longer if it was a finger or a tongue.

"I want to fuck you in the ass, but I can't when you're tied up!" Matt worked another finger into her pussy, feeling her stretch around him, and plunged them forward, his hand rocking with her body. He knew that it wouldn't be long before she came again. His own heart beat rapidly as sweat poured down his face.

Lucy screamed for the second time that night as yet another orgasm burned through her lower body. She jerked against him, grunting out her enjoyment. When the pulses slowed, her body went limp on the surface of the bed. Perspiration dampened her forehead as she lay with her eyes closed behind the blindfold.

Matt's fingers left her pussy, but the pressure of his finger in her ass remained. Again, warm lips tugs at her swollen clit.

Lucy's lower body shuddered against his mouth, and she whimpered again from behind her blindfold. "You're driving me wild, Matt. I want your cock in me! Please! Please, you've got to stop! "

A muffled chuckle met her ears just before the finger in her anus began to pump, whipping the heat inside of her again. "You bastard!" She arched again, her hips leaving the bed and with the muscles of her rectum squeezing around the finger that drove her insane. "Fuck me, you bastard. Fuck me with your cock! Please!"

Suddenly the pressure in her ass subsided. Matt crawled up her body. Her heart pounded when the fullness of his cock slide into her wet heat. He filled her completely as her body expanded around him. His hips began to thrust; hard, solid strokes that caused his cock to throb against her cervix, urging her to join him in yet another wild and wondrous ride.

He slid in and out of her raised body on the pillow, slamming harder each time he glided through her hot length. A full two minutes passed before his strokes shortened, signaling the waiting orgasm that built in his groin.

Lucy clenched around him; over and over her body pulsed as the biggest orgasm of the night rolled through her like a thunderstorm. She screamed and bit his shoulder as hot cum filled her body.

Chapter Thirteen: The Other Half

Lucy rolled to her side in the bed, pulled her knees to her bare chest, and stared through the window at the morning sun. Her body still ached with the pleasure Matt bestowed on her the evening before. But the thought of how he had tenderly untied her, removed the blindfold and spooned around her body just before she fell asleep sent a river of pain through her heart. He would probably never warm her bed again. He'd left for home only an hour earlier to change into work clothes and head for the project site.

She flipped to her back, her poignant gaze now following a spider that skittered across the ceiling, hurrying to find a dark place to hide from the brightness of the day. She squeezed her eyelids shut. *What am I going to do? I can't let them get by with what they did to me.* But as she searched for the emotion of revenge, only love burned behind her lids in the form of tears.

Lucy dragged her legs over the edge of the bed and wiped away the tear that escaped down her cheek. She couldn't let the emotions that ran through her heart rule her brain. Matt and Jake had played a horrible joke on her and, even though she let that fact go as Matt teased her body through one orgasm after another, she had to make them pay.

Trudging through the door and down the hallway, she entered the bathroom and turned on the shower. The hot water would clear her head and sooth her aching body.

What now? She vigorously scrubbed her lean body with a washcloth, leaving red marks trailing across her skin wherever she touched. *Put it in order, Lucy. First, you have to find Jake and mess with his mind.* Last night she thought that's what she had accomplished with Matt during supper. She knew he was extremely upset as she continually prodded him with reminders of her sessions with Jake. *But the joke was on me. The son of a bitch turned the tables and left me a quivering mass…*

They had slept for an hour or two, and then Matt had continued to make passionate love to her throughout the entire night. Just thinking of it now caused a shiver to run up her spine and her pussy to become wet. *But it has to stop! Think of the future! Can you imagine spending holidays with the two of them knowing what they tried to pull?*

And what about Jake? Lucy leaned against the wall of the shower stall and let the hot water run down her body as she examined her feelings. Twice he had made love to her. Not just a quick fuck, but loving, hot sessions worthy to be remembered years from now. At the time, she thought she was in love with him. She was — no she wasn't. *You thought you were with Matt, not Jake. That's why you told him you loved him…*

Lucy groaned loudly as she ran her fingers through her wet hair, tipped her neck back, and rested her head against the wall. "I did love the man I was with," she mumbled to the tiled walls. "Whether it was Matt or Jake…" She sighed. "I loved the person who touched me tenderly. I loved the person who—"

Her body stiffened. *I loved the person who said they loved me!* Both men had declared their feelings. Why would Jake say he loved her when there wasn't any need to?

She needed to find out. Lucy grabbed the shampoo, squirted a dollop into her waiting palm, and smeared it through her hair. Her fingers moved quickly to help rinse the suds out of the long strands. A quick rinse and her body was squeaky clean.

Hopping out of the shower, ignoring her small aches and pains, Lucy hurried to her room as she blotted the water from her skin. She had to find Jake. Her shift didn't start until 6:00 tonight, giving her the entire day to wreak havoc. Somehow, she had to figure out where he was, continue with the second part of her revenge while trying to discover his true feelings as far as she was concerned. Only then, could she make a final decision about the two men.

* * * * *

She drove around town searching for his truck. It was easy to remember because of the fire-red color, big tires, and the metal running boards mounted below each door. She had watched it in her rearview mirror chasing her for eight blocks only a few days earlier.

Twice she had driven by the school to see if it was parked anywhere, not the least concerned if Matt saw her. He would continue to work throughout the day as he always did. *Remember, Lucy, he always works during the day. It's Jake who pretends to be the one running an errand!*

And then it hit her. "Stupid! Stupid! Stupid!" She pulled to the side of the road, glanced over her shoulder, and did a U-turn, accelerating in the direction of Matt's apartment.

Five minutes later, she spotted the truck parked in the driveway. Lucy drove right on by, her fingers curled around the steering wheel with determination as she headed for the café.

Slamming her car into Park, she bounded from behind the wheel and ran across the main street.

Mavis watched the young woman race through the doorway and behind the counter. "What's the hurry? You don't come on shift until tonight."

Lucy pulled a fresh baked pie from the glass cabinet, dropped it on the counter and bent to yank a Styrofoam container from one of the shelves. "I need a piece of pie."

Mavis leaned against the counter at the far end, observed when the first piece landed upside down on the floor, and shook her head at the mild expletive that left Lucy's mouth as she bent to clean up the mess with a pile of napkins. "Slow down, Luce. Where's the fire?"

"I've got to hurry before Jake leaves Matt's apartment. This is the excuse I need to get in the door."

"What the hell are you up to now?"

Lucy flipped the lid shut on the container. "The second part of my revenge. I'm going to drive those two crazy before I'm finished with them." She scooped up the pie tin and shoved it back inside the glass enclosure.

"Stop right there!" Mavis waddled her girth across the floor and grabbed the young woman by the arm. "What are you thinking? You're going to get hurt."

"I already am."

"Well, then, go talk to Matt. Tell him what you know and get answers to your questions."

Lucy's head shook stubbornly. "No way. I'm going to have my fun with them first. Then I just might tell them both to go to hell." She rounded the counter with a nod of her chin. "I'll see you tonight."

Mavis shook her head, turned, and finished cleaning the mess left in Lucy's wake.

* * * * *

Jake's truck was still in the driveway. Lucy took a deep breath, fingered Matt's apartment key in her pocket, and entered the building with the pie in her hand. Instead of waiting for the elevator, she raced up the steps that led to the second floor. Two more turns and she was standing before his door. She breathed deeply to calm her nerves, inserted the key, and shoved the door open.

Jake stood in his underwear, frying himself breakfast as he kept one eye on the small television perched on the snack bar. Hearing the door, he turned to ask Matt why he was back.

The sight of Lucy standing with her auburn hair curling around her face nearly buckled his knees. "Lucy? What are you doing here?"

"Oh! Matt!" Her free hand fluttered across her chest as she played the part of being surprised. "Geez! You scared me. I didn't expect to see you here." Her eyes inspected his bare chest from across the room. She was too far away to see if the little scar was present. She had to be sure.

Lucy dropped her purse on the coffee table as she made her way to the kitchen. "I was down visiting Mavis. I know how much you like apple pie," she held the container up, "so I grabbed a fresh piece and was going to leave it as a surprise for when you got home tonight." Her eyes scanned his scantily clad length. "But it looks like I'm going to get the surprise!"

Placing the pie on the snack bar, she strolled around the squared end and sidled up to him. Her eyes rested on his chest. The scar was like an emblazoned red letter A on his chest. *'A' for asshole,* she thought. *Let the show begin…*

Her arms reached up to surround his broad shoulders as she pulled him close. "Hmmm…thank you for the wonderful night last night. I don't think I've ever come as many times as that. You were great!"

Jake reached tentative arms around her small waist, his brain racing. The only thing he could come up with was, "It was my pleasure. You make it easy for me to be good."

Lucy rolled her eyes at his response as she stood with her cheek against his bare chest. Nuzzling his firm breast, she sighed loudly. "Do you have to go to work, or would you like a little morning dessert before your eggs?"

"Oh, shit!" Jake's arms left her waist as he spun to move the pan to a cold burner. The eggs were ruined. He didn't give a shit. Eggs were the last things he wanted—especially with Lucy in the room. But he had to get rid of her.

Up until yesterday, he and Matt had never had so much as an argument. His brother had come home early this morning from spending the night with Lucy, whistling with happiness and ready to make peace. He and Matt had had a long talk, discussing both their guilt when it came to having duped Lucy.

As hurt as he was, his and Jake's special connection through their many years wasn't something that could be tossed callously aside. Matt admitted his own guilt and told Jake he could live with it. Jake swore to never touch Lucy again. He suddenly realized it wasn't going to be that easy.

Trying to remain calm, he placed his hands on her shoulders and smiled. "As much as I'd like to stay, I really have to get to work."

You damned liar! Well, I've got other plans for you... Her finger curled in the wiry hair of his chest. It was all she could do to keep from rubbing it across the little scar. "Really? I couldn't convince you to stay and play for just a little while?"

Jake's jaw clenched. *Matt has created a monster – one I'd like to be lying inside right now.* He shook his head. "Who would run the show? There's a lot to get done today."

"You're telling me!"

Before Jake knew what was happening, Lucy slid her fingers into the waistband of his boxers and yanked them down past his knees in one swell swoop.

"Hey!"

She dropped to the floor on her knees, nuzzled her face against his growing erection, and wrapped her lips around his penis, coaxing it to stand tall. It did.

Jake tried to back away, but the stove stopped his retreat. He was trapped between the cold stainless steel against his bare ass and the hot, wet lips wrapped around his penis. His stomach sucked in when her hand slid up the inside of his thigh to caress his balls. "Lucy..."

Her mouth left his cock only for a moment as she gazed up, using her fingers wrapped around his staff to keep him a prisoner. "Just let me give you a blowjob before you leave. If you don't want to fuck me when I'm done, I'll understand and let you leave for work." Her tongue darted out to swirl around his glistening head. "Matt, honey—you were so wonderful last night. I loved being tied down and having you do all those soft things to me. I think that was the best session we've had yet. It was so different from the night of the reunion."

Jake frowned. *Matt tied her up?*

"I just find it hard when comparing those two times." She flicked her tongue against his cock and smiled to herself when he jerked slightly. "It's as if two different men had made love to me, but I know that's not possible. "

Jake swallowed with enormous guilt, but the probing tongue against his length kept him from pushing Lucy away.

"Just this morning," she whispered between gentle sucks, "I was wondering which type of lovemaking I liked best. I can't decide. When you're gentle, you're soooo good!"

Keep that up, Lucy, and I'll show you how good rough-fucking can be...

"So, will you let me finish this blowjob? Like I said, I'll understand if you can't stay for more." Her mouth returned to his erection to tease him into acceptance of her proposition. She sucked hard and took his entire length into her mouth.

Jake's hands curled around the edge of the stove. His head fell back as his hips automatically surged forward to push his penis even further into her mouth. "Christ..." he muttered. Lucy sucked in earnest now, keeping him pinned against the stove. "I...can't..." She sucked harder, her head bobbing up and down the length of him. "Fuck..." Heat curled in his belly like a poisonous snake. Jake grabbed her head with his hands, moving his hips away from the stove as she stroked him with her hand and wiggled her tongue against the slit of his penis.

The only sound in the kitchen was his heavy breathing and a slurping sound as she devoured his cock. Sparks lit his groin on fire as she fanned the flames higher with her tonguing actions.

Lucy smiled to herself at how easily she had gotten him to forget anything else but her. And now? His hips surged forward, seeking for more of what she could give him—plus, she would be the one to benefit when he tried to prove, if only to himself, that he was the better lover. The power she felt built her confidence. Sliding her hands up and around his ass, she urged him further into her mouth, ran the line of his ass crack with her fingers, and inserted a slim finger into his anus.

Jake jerked forward again, a deep growl sounded in his throat, and he spewed cum into her mouth.

Lucy lapped at him, swallowing as her finger moved in and out of his rectum. She continued to suck him even as the final blasts of cum ended.

Jake yanked her to her feet, scooped her into his arms and headed for the bedroom. Tossing her onto her back, his hands hauled her white t-shirt over head. Her bra followed a second later. Just as quickly, her pants were opened and jerked down over her long legs.

Lucy shoved her thong down past her thighs before her ankles were freed from her jeans. Her hot gaze found his crotch where his cock was already hardening up before her eyes.

Jake flopped beside her naked body and dragged her across his chest. His eyes narrowed dangerously as he stared into her smoldering ones—a warning that she had started something that he damn well was going to finish. "You drive me nuts, lady. I can't say no to you."

Lucy slithered across the top of him, using her body to caress the erection between them. "Then don't."

Jake shoved her off him and onto her back, yanked her legs open, and crammed his finger into her dripping pussy. His teeth found her erect nipples, and then moved to nip her breasts as he shoved another finger into her as deep as he could. "Fuck...I can't get far enough into you."

Lucy bucked beneath his hand and spread her legs wider. Jerking his head down, she pushed his face past her stomach and between her thighs.

Jake scrambled to find a better position as he lapped at her clit, his fingers still filling her tunnel as she wiggled tighter against his mouth. Not being able to wait a moment longer to feel her wet heat around him, he reared up and pinned her to the bed with his cock, slamming into her as the bed shook around them.

Lucy met each thrust with wild grunts and murmurs beside his ear, which only spurred him on. He was crazy for her, blocking out anything but the feel of her hot sheath around him and the smell of sex in the air. Suddenly, being wrapped inside her slick heat wasn't enough.

He pulled out, rolled her to her stomach and yanked her ass up. Jake easily slid his wet cock up her ass. Immediately, the two found the tempo they craved and the bed began to clatter against the wall.

Lucy braced her elbows, threw her head back, and thrust against him. Her ass jiggled each time he slammed into her. She screamed when the rolling orgasm hit her, and collapsed to the surface of the bed, her legs still spread wide to allow him all the access he needed.

Jake followed her down and continued to pump into her tight hole, his back drenched with perspiration. Suddenly, he impaled himself within her and came again with a shudder into her ass.

He rolled from her body and landed on his back, barely aware when she crawled closer to lay her head on his heaving chest. Lucy kissed the small jagged scar before she drew a deep breath to calm her racing heart.

The flick of her tongue brought him back to the present. He snaked an arm around her shoulders and pulled her closer; his hand caressed her soft upper arm.

Lucy's whisper trickled across his heart. "I love you, Matt."

Jake tightened his grip, wishing that it were his name on her lips. "God help me, I love you, too."

Chapter Fourteen: The Sting

Lucy curled her legs beneath her and cuddled into the back of her padded porch swing. Sipping at the hot cup of tea she held in her hands, she sighed heavily. Things weren't going as planned. What she desired was to make both Matt and Jake pay for their hijinks. Instead, she found herself craving both men; Matt with his sweet temperament and ability to coax an orgasm from her without even entering her body; and Jake who took control of any situation and made her body sing as he nipped and pounded with all his might.

The joke was on her. Lucy was acutely aware that there was a good possibility she was in love with two brothers. And as much as the building wish in her heart was to be with the both of them, settling the score still burned bright.

Her face dropped into her upturned palms. Only heartache could come from this entire mess she had secretly manipulated, and she would be the one to carry the heaviest load.

She stiffened. *But they started it! They were the ones who tried to pull the wool over my eyes.* Lucy bounded from the swing, wanting to slam her fist against the side of the house. She whipped open the door and headed up the stairs to change for work.

As she jerked her t-shirt off and kicked her pants to the floor, the seed of a retribution plan began to develop in her head. Lucy stood in the middle of the room with her uniform in her hand and stared at herself in the mirror. She needed to confront both of them at the same time and then walk away with her head held high.

She was working the morning shift the next day. Having to be at the café on back-to-back shifts would make planning difficult, but if she was going to get revenge, it needed to be done quickly—for more reasons than one. First, there would be a good chance that Jake would leave for wherever his home was and getting the two men together might never happen after that. Secondly, Lucy was sinking slowly into the web they had all created. If she didn't get out soon, the heartache would only get worse. With a firm streak of resolve running down her spine, Lucy slipped her uniform over her head and ignored the pain that had settled in her chest.

✳ ✳ ✳ ✳ ✳

"I'm going to take a break, Mavis," she called over her shoulder as she dug through some of her tip money jingling in her pocket. "I've got a few personal calls to make." It was Wednesday morning and Lucy's breakfast crowd had finally finished up and was heading out the café door.

Glancing one more time around the half-empty diner to assure herself that no one was within hearing distance, she crossed to the pay phone and dropped a quarter into the slot, dialed a number that she had memorized, and waited for someone to answer.

"Colby Hotel. How may I be of service?"

"Ah…hi. I'd like to rent a room please? Well, actually, I'd like to reserve adjoining hot tub suites if that's possible."

"And what date would you like to arrive?"

"Um…I know this is kind of last minute, but would it be possible to reserve them tonight?"

"Please hold one moment and I'll check to see if anything is available."

The sound of piano music filtered through the handset as Lucy waited impatiently and fiddled with a crooked menu board near the front door.

"Hello?"

"I'm here!"

"You're in luck. The adjoining suites are open. Now, if you would have called for them this weekend, they wouldn't have been open."

Lucy rolled her eyes. She didn't care about this weekend — she cared about tonight. Her finger traced a pattern around the edge of the frame. "Okay, then, I'd like to reserve one of the rooms under the name of Matt Diamond and the other under Lucy O'Malley, but I'll give you one credit card number to hold both. Would that be possible? There will be two separate groups arriving at separate times."

"No problem. Will you need a key for the adjoining rooms so both parties may visit each other?"

Lucy's hand jerked at the question. The menu board flipped off the wall and clattered to the floor. She caught Mavis' shaking head in her peripheral vision and quickly leaned the board upright against the wall.

"Yes. Yes, I'll need that key also."

"All right, then, I'll need your credit card number to hold these rooms. Check-in is after one o'clock."

Lucy slid the plastic card from her pocket, read off the number, and listened to the rehearsed thank you speech from the voice on the other end of the line. This was working out better than she hoped. Two o'clock was the end of her shift. After she hung up, she inserted another quarter and dialed Matt's cell number. First, she would need to make sure that he was at work and not at the apartment.

"Hello, Lucy!"

"Matt! You knew it was me."

"The restaurant number came up on the screen. How's it going, baby?"

"Good...it's been a little busy, but I finally found the time to call you." She paused for a moment, took a deep breath, and knew if she didn't ask him now, she would lose her nerve for tonight. "Matt? I've got a surprise planned for us. I feel bad that

I asked you not to come to my house last night. My head was pounding and I just needed to sleep. The only thing is this. I want to pick you up at the work site. I'm sorry, but you won't be able to go home first." She had to keep the two men apart.

"That's an intriguing offer. What do you have planned?"

She glanced up at the ceiling and swallowed down her nervousness. "Uh-uh, it's a surprise. I get off at two o'clock. I'll come straight to the school and get you. You can get off early, can't you? I can't wait for you to see what I have planned."

"Yeah, I think I can swing it."

"Great!" her brain whirred with something else to say. Before she'd discovered the Diamond boy's deception, conversation always came easy. Now she was struggling. *Think, Lucy!* "Eat a good lunch, hon, because I'm horny and you're going to need your strength." *There. That ought to keep him in a constant state of hard-on…*

"You tease! All right, I'm up already just thinking about it!" His chuckle echoed in her ear.

"I have a customer, so I'll see you about two fifteen."

"Okay! Love you, Luce."

Her lids squeezed shut as she gripped the phone with white fingers. "I love you, too. Bye."

She hung up and fished for another quarter with shaking hands. A second later, she was dialing Matt's home phone. "Come on, please be there…" The phone rang a third time.

"Hello?"

Lucy's heart did a flip. "Hi, Matt! This is Lucy."

"Ah…hi, Lucy." There was a slight pause. *"What's up?"*

"Hopefully you." Lucy winced. Her audacity even surprised her at times. She could only hear the sound of his breathing. "I wanted to do something special. My treat. I really want to see you, and I want to do it in a particular surrounding. I rented a room at the Colby Inn and wanted to know if you could meet me there. Just think. Hot tub, wine and cheese and, most importantly, just you and me naked with no phones and no way for anyone to find us. What do you think?"

Lucy would never know that Jake dropped to a chair, flabbergasted at the opportunity she had just offered him. There was no way he would be able to pull it off without Matt asking him where he'd been, but he couldn't stop the words that tumbled from his mouth.

"When were you planning this little shindig?"

"Well, you see, that's the thing. The Colby Inn has this special, but we'd have to take the opportunity like now. If you could be there by one to check in, we won't lose the room. I can't be there until closer to three, but what the hell? Take a nice long shower and watch some sports until I get there."

"I don't know..."

"I want you naked and hard, sweetie. When I get there, I want you lying in bed with a hard-on that will make me drool." The intake of breath on the other end was harsh.

"You've got me hard just thinking about it."

"Please, Matt? I've got an afternoon of sex planned that will leave you begging for more! We don't even have to stay the night."

"You're pretty persuasive. All right. Do you want me to bring anything?"

"Yeah, yourself. Everything else will be there. Ask for the room in my name."

* * * * *

Jake inserted the card into the lock and waited for the light to turn green. A flick of the wrist later, and he entered the suite.

A low whistle left his lips. The room was gorgeous, with a king-size bed up against the wall. A gas fireplace hugged the corner. A hot tub big enough for two people perched beside it. This was a room for sex.

He tossed a small duffle bag on the chair and crossed to the television. "Hell, what more could a man want!" He shoved away the guilt his spoken words elicited—the guilt that had eaten at him since he agreed to meet Lucy—and clicked on the TV. Matt need never know about this rendezvous. If he did discover this little tryst, however, he planned to tell his brother how he'd fallen in love with the crazy redhead, too. "What a damned predicament the three of us are in..." He stretched out on the bed, placed his hands behind his head, and stared at the ceiling. He had an hour before he needed to strip, take a shower, and be ready for the little minx to appear.

* * * * *

Matt pressed Lucy against the flat surface of the suite door and kissed her deeply. She giggled when his hand dropped to cup her breast and tried to remain calm.

"Hey! What if someone sees us? Let's go inside." Lucy was concerned that for some reason, Jake would open the hallway door only twenty feet away and her plan would be kaput. She had called his room before leaving the café to pick up Matt. He hadn't disappointed her. Jake was there and promised to be naked and ready for her. She wiggled the room card before Matt's nose and waited for him to take the hint.

Once the door was open, Matt hurried her inside as his gaze did a quick scan of the fireplace and Jacuzzi. "Wow! Great room. I think my guilt for leaving work early just disappeared into thin air. His hand reached for the top button of her shirt, but Lucy clasped his fingers and halted his hand when it dropped to the second.

"This is your treat, Matt. I've thought about you naked all day. Let me start." She stood on her tiptoes and kissed his lips softly to set the tone. The last thing she wanted was for them to rush to get naked and climb into bed. If that happened, it would mess up everything. Her hand fluttered to his waist where she grabbed the material of his tucked-in t-shirt and pulled it slowly from his pants. Matt lifted his bulging arms when she pulled his top over his head.

She knew he was not going to fight her suggestion when his arms dropped, and he waited for her to unzip his jeans. Lucy ran her tongue slowly over her top lip as she smiled, unbuttoned his flap and worked the zipper down over his bulging erection. "Hmmm...I see you're very ready for me. I think, though, that you're going to have to let me play with you a little first."

Matt tipped his chin and bussed her cheek softly as she worked the jeans over his slim hips. "How was I so lucky to find someone like you?"

Lucy almost turned tail and ran. She refused to look up at him as she waited for him to step out of his pants. *You won't be thinking that shortly.*

She felt like crying. As much as she wanted this revenge, a bigger part of her wanted to take him in her arms and hold him close. The problem was, however, that his twin brother was waiting for her in the adjoining room and she yearned to do the same thing to him.

As she worked Matt's boxers over his penis and down his legs, she suppressed a shudder of sadness that threatened to overwhelm her. *Lucy and her double Diamonds... Diamonds aren't a girl's best friend...double love...I'm a sick person to think I could pull this off...*

She took a deep breath of courage. She wouldn't stop now. Even though a wave of desire for the two men hit her with the force of a hurricane, she had to keep going. It was a horrible trick they played—and it was horrible that she discovered that she loved them both. Too late. There wasn't a thing she could do about it anyway except to reveal her knowledge of their deception and walk away. Matt and Jake were a pair. If she couldn't have one, then she couldn't have the other.

Lucy rose and hugged Matt tightly. His erection bumped against her with a quiet urgent need that she ignored. She would play the part, however.

Her hand dropped to caress him. She wanted to assure that he would remain hard while the second part of her plan played out. Applying a slight pressure of her hand against his cock, she walked him backwards to the edge of the bed.

Matt sat with his legs spread, waiting to see what she would do next. Hope and desire lit his gaze as he looked up. "God, I hope you're going to do what I think you are." He leaned back and rested his palms flat on the surface of the bed, waiting for her to sink to her knees.

Lucy's smile hurt her face. Glancing down at his cock, she reached out to stroke him gently. "Can't wait for my lips around this, can you?"

"Quit teasing me, Luce. You've got me worked up into quite a state."

"You're going to be even more worked up when I'm through with you. Wait right here." She strolled to the small fridge and opened the door. "Oh, shoot. The management must have put the whipped cream in the other room." She turned and saw the confusion in his eyes.

"What other room?"

"The special offer was two adjoining suite rooms. Once we're done here, we can go next door and…" she lifted her hands with a leering smile and a shrug of her shoulders, "…then we can do it all over again. No! Stay right there!"

Matt settled his naked ass back on the bedspread. His cock throbbed to be sucked.

"You stay right there. Keep that baby hard. I'm going to run next door and get the whipped cream. When I come back, I plan to squirt it all over you and lick it off."

His broad chest dropped with a whoosh of air. Just when he thought they'd done it all, Lucy had come up with another fun session of sex.

"I'm not going anywhere. And I don't think we have to worry about me going soft."

"Good! I'll be right back." She pulled another plastic card from her back pocket, squeezed her breasts for his enjoyment, and then continued across the room to the adjoining door. A moment later, she disappeared and closed the door behind her.

* * * * *

Jake lay beneath the bedspread with two pillows propped behind his back. He was buck assed naked and got an instant hard-on when Lucy walked through the door.

"I've been waiting for you. Wait a minute…what the heck are you doing coming through that door?"

She licked her lips with a smile, however hard she found it to keep up the pretense. The stress of getting them together was starting to wear on her nerves. Thank goodness Jake had hit his cue. He was naked as she had asked him to be. "I forgot to tell you that we've got two adjoining suites. That was the deal." She walked closer, bent to hold his hands against the bed, and dropped her lips to kiss the small scar. "I can't wait to feel you sliding into me. Are you big and hard?" Her hand found his crotch beneath the blanket. His cock was rigid and waiting.

Lucy glanced about the room and rested her gaze on the hot tub. "You know what? The hot tub in the other room is bigger. Let's go in there. Then I want you to strip me naked and fuck me in the ass."

His penis bobbed with excitement in her hand. Jake wrapped his large hand around the back of her head and pulled her mouth to his. His tongue slashed across the seam of her lips, forcing them open to admit him inside. "You don't know what you do to me, woman."

No, but you will – and it's breaking my heart... "So, come on, big guy. Let's get started," she mumbled against his mouth.

Jake scrambled from the bed, his erection as big and hard as his brother's only a short walk away. Lucy pulled him across the room to the door, rested her hand on the handle, and nodded before she pulled it open. "You go first. I want to watch your great set of buns walking in front of me." She pulled on the handle.

Jake smiled and stepped through the doorway.

Chapter Fifteen: Mirror, Mirror On the Wall

"What the fuck..." Jake's penis went limp faster than if someone had smacked him in the balls. His dropped jaw mirrored Matt's, who leapt from the bed and dragged the bedspread across the front of his naked body as his erection deflated.

The two brothers stared at each other, a myriad of emotions passing over their surprised faces.

Lucy strutted into the room, glanced at Matt who had covered himself, and grabbed a menu from the table. Jake flinched when she bounced it off his limp cock and held it there. "Well, take it. As long as your brother doesn't want his dick hanging out for everyone to see, you may as well cover yours also." Jake grabbed it from her fingers and sank into a chair.

Matt shuffled his stance, anger blazing from deep inside his gaze. "What the fuck's going on here, Lucy?"

"You tell me," she shot back. The voice of a sportscaster from the television in the next filtered through the doorway. It was the only sound as all three stared at one another. Lucy leaned against the dresser, simply amazed that she had pulled her plan off without making a bumbling mess of things. "Well, since you are both tongue-tied, let me begin. I think both of you are fucking idiots. When I found out how the two of you were fooling me into believing you were one person..."

"Wait one minute." Matt's anger subsided slightly when he interrupted her. No matter how Lucy tried to act the part of the uncaring woman, the hurt blazed in her emerald eyes. He'd beat the hell out of his brother later. For now, he felt like a heel — a heel who looked like he was going to lose the woman he loved. "How long have you known?"

"Long enough to fuck both of you and know that it was a different man I was with and not the Matt that I first fell in love with."

Both men winced. "Lucy..." Matt started again.

"Don't you *Lucy* me!" she jumped forward and slashed her finger through the air at both of them. "Shame on the two of you! Shame on you for taking my emotions *and* my body and doing the things that you did! What is this? Some sick game you two play because no one can tell the two of you apart? What?" She looked frantically around the room, trying to get her thoughts in order. She glared at Matt. "Did you fuck me and then wait for Jake to have his turn so you two could get together and compare stories?"

"It wasn't like that," Jake spoke from his chair.

She spun on her heel and glared at him. Her heart pounded with anger and with the loss she was having a hard time facing. "Then you tell me what the hell it was! How long was this going to go on if I hadn't discovered the truth?"

"Yes, tell us, Jake," Matt gritted out. "You promised me never to touch her again."

"Oh, shut up, Matt," Lucy spewed. "You act like you're the hurt party here!" she jabbed her chest with her finger. "I'm the one whose emotions were brutalized by this. I'm the one who was used by the two of you!" She crossed her arms over her chest as the quiet continued after her outburst. "Well, one of you say something. Before I leave this room, I want to know the truth about how this happened." To her, both men looked ill as one waited for the other to speak.

Matt tightened the bedspread around his lower body and dropped to the bed with a sigh. "I'm sorry, Lucy. It was my idea."

"You bastard," she hissed quietly.

Her two words cut him to the quick. He wasn't about to disagree. Matt's shoulders dropped with the huge sigh that left his mouth. "It started on the night of the reunion. I was getting ready to go home and clean up." His gaze shifted to his brother who sat quietly in the chair with the menu across his lap. If the entire situation hadn't been so horrible, Matt would have burst out laughing. "Jake showed up with a woman from my past. I can't believe I had actually lived with her at one time. You can believe what you want, but Stephanie is crazy. That's why I finally ended things with her, took this job, and got the hell out of Milwaukee so she couldn't find me." He waited for Lucy to say something—anything to get his mind off the look of pain in her eyes. He knew how talk about Steph had deflated her growing confidence over the past few months. "I knew how excited you were to attend your reunion—it's the only thing you talked about for weeks."

Lucy turned her head away from him and stared at Jake, whose cheek clenched and unclenched beneath her stiff and unbending perusal. "And why would you bring this person with you? Did you want her to get back together with Matt?"

"Hell, no!" Jake made to scoot forward to the edge of the chair and realized his predicament with the menu. He simply tightened his fingers around the plastic edges, pressed it closer to his groin, and leaned back to stay put. "She had discovered where Matt was and was heading up here to find him. She is nuts, Lucy. I didn't want him surprised—I tried calling him, but he never got my messages. I figured I'd ride along to play referee. Honest to God, Matt wanted nothing to do with her."

"Why should he?" was her flippant comeback. "He was fucking me—someone who was stupid enough to believe the loving drivel that dripped from his mouth."

Matt's head slumped, making Lucy yearn to snatch back the comment.

Jake charged on. "Steph would have gone looking for you if Matt would've kicked her off the project site. He didn't want the two of you meeting up. She stated between sneers and tears that if he would pay off some of her debts and give her a ride back to Milwaukee, then she would walk out of his life and stay out.

That's all he wanted from her. To be gone—because he loves you."

Lucy's frazzled mind worked overtime. "So the two of you simply thought you'd pull a switch on me and I would be none the wiser." She turned back to look at Matt. "Did it ever cross your mind that I would want you to come home with me that night?"

He nodded, and then swallowed. "Jake was supposed to get you drunk."

"He did."

"Drunk enough to pass out."

"Well, boys, I guess I can hold my liquor, can't I?"

Jake shrugged. "Lucy, I never planned to make love to you. In fact, I tried to tell you no—more than once, but you're too damned persuasive. I tried, but I couldn't stop myself."

Her gaze softened as she continued to stare. "So why did we make love again? Why did you take me home that morning we met in front of the café and make love to me, especially when you knew this Steph person was out of the way? When I came to the apartment, I knew who you really were. You had a chance to tell me then—you had a chance to send me home."

Matt leaned forward waiting for his brother's answer. Apparently the two had been together more times than he knew about. He waited for the green head of jealousy to rear up inside of him. It didn't. Looking at Jake's face, he suddenly knew what the answer would be, but wanted to hear the words from his lips.

Jake ran his free hand through his thick hair, stared hard at his brother, and inhaled deeply. "Because, Lucy, you did to me what you did to Matt. You worked your way into my heart, and I fell in love with you before I knew it was even happening."

Her fingers covered her mouth as she snapped her lids shut. Her brain blurred as stars spun in her head. She reached behind her to hang onto the dresser and steady herself. The situation was impossible. She was in love with two handsome brothers—her double diamonds—she wouldn't fool herself into believing something else that wasn't true. And they were both in love with her.

Matt shuffled the blanket in his lap, looking from one to the other. Lucy had her eyes shut as she grasped the dresser behind her. Jake clutched his menu, looking sicker by the minute. How could he be upset with either of them for making love? He was the person guilty of throwing them together in an almost impossible situation. He loved them both. Jake was an essential part of his life—always had been—always would be.

His eyes shifted back to Lucy who now stared at the carpet, her shoulders slumped, and confusion written all over her face. How would he be able to make it through his days if she wasn't at his side at night? He had a lot to think about. "Lucy?"

Her chin came up slowly. Tears twinkled in her eyes as she batted them away.

"I love you. I don't know how we're going to fix this, but I don't want to lose you. I'm sorry that we had to get to this point. It was a stupid idea that I'll regret forever."

Her head shook slowly as she ran both hands through her hair starting at the temples and ending with clamped fingers behind her slim neck. She squeezed her eyes tightly and winced. Both men watched her closely.

Finally, she met their stares with a sad look. "Why does this have to be so hard? Why did you both do this to me? I'm going to be honest—something that maybe the two of you should try. Once I found out that I actually had two men in my life, I decided on revenge. And contrary to what everyone says, it's not sweet. I tried to pit the two of you together to get under your skin because I was so pissed and hurt. What happened though, is the two of you got under mine. I'm sorry, Matt, but at some point when I thought I was loving you, but it was actually Jake, I think I fell in love with your brother." Jake's head snapped up.

Lucy pushed herself away from the dresser and picked up her purse. "Well, isn't this going to be something to enter into my diary? Lucy's double Diamonds. Hmmm...double the trouble and double the misery." She slung the strap over her shoulder and reached for the hallway door. "By the way. You two owe for this 'double' room. Isn't that funny?"

Chapter Sixteen: The Proposal

The delivery boy from Anderson's Floral Shoppe shoved another bouquet of flowers across the counter with a smile creasing his face. "You sure have one heck of an admirer, Luce. You gonna keep this one?" He waited to see what she was going to do this time.

Lucy casually picked up the vase of fragrant flowers, took three steps, and dropped the entire arrangement into the garbage, just as she had every bouquet she'd received daily for the last three weeks. She dusted her hands together and continued emptying the tray of clean glasses.

Mavis sat at the end of the counter, totaling up her tips for the day with a shake of her head. "You could at least look at the card."

"I don't have to look at it. I never asked for them and I could give a shit less." She glanced over her shoulder at the delivery boy. "Don't waste your time coming with more tomorrow, Mickey. If an order comes in, just drop whatever it is into the dumpster at the floral shop."

Mickey cackled as he rose from the stool. "Just doing my job, Luce." He glanced at his watch. "Well, guess I better be hitting the road. I've got three more stops to make. See you tomorrow!"

"Smart ass," Lucy mumbled beneath her breath. The bell tinkled over Mickey's head as he left the café.

Mavis heaved her bulk up, rolled the one-dollar bills into a wad, and shoved them into her pocket. "You ever going to forgive Matt?"

"He can kiss my ass."

"I bet he'd like to about now."

Lucy ignored her comment and prepared to leave for the day.

Mavis decided to try again. "He made a mistake. People do that sometimes. You should really give him a call and let him explain."

The younger woman shrugged as she counted out her tip money, eager to be home to lick her wounds through yet another night of loneliness. Mavis didn't know that Lucy had already received her explanation the night she left Matt and Jake sitting naked in a hotel room, and Lucy was perfectly happy to leave it that way. Discussing the entire situation out loud would only make her cry again—and she'd managed to stave off the tears for three nights running now—an achievement in itself considering how low she felt. "I don't want to talk about it, Mavis. You want to go to a movie or something tonight? Or maybe even stop for a beer—or a keg of beer." A sad, forced smile touched her lips. "We don't have to work in the morning."

Shrugging on a sweater, Mavis gathered her purse from behind the counter. "Sounds good, but not tonight. I think Frank's coming over for a little slap and tickle."

Lucy couldn't help but smile—her first real smile since she walked out on the two men in her life. Correction—the two men who used to be in her life. "Okay. I guess I'll see you in a couple of days. If you want to do something tomorrow, just give me a call."

Mavis shook her head again. "Why in hell would you want to spend a day off with an old lady? You ought to be with people your own age—or with Matt."

Lucy shook her head and decided to leave without any more invitations. Mavis had been chewing on her ass for three weeks now about making peace with Matt and she wasn't in the mood to listen to it anymore. She left the restaurant, telling herself she was glad to have a few days off. Since the breakup, she'd taken every extra shift she could simply to not spend time mooning over that fact that she was heartbroken, lonely, and craving the hot touch of both Diamond brothers.

After a quick stop at the store for cat food, Lucy drove the long way home, stopping at the city park to feed the ducks, to enjoy the warm evening, and to figure out what the hell she was going to do with the rest of her life. The realization that she didn't want to go home to an empty house hit her. When she was with Matt, she'd rush home to be welcomed into his arms if he was there, or wait excitedly on the porch for his Suburban to drive up. Now, she had nothing but Mr. Pibbs' continual meowing because he wanted his dinner. She would have to contend with the fact that she missed both Matt and Jake.

Forcing herself up from the bench, she trudged back to her car and headed for home and another boring night.

She drove back across town and turned up the last street. Her home was at the very end of the block. As she drove closer, she straightened behind the wheel, curled her fingers around the hard plastic in a death grip, and swore beneath her breath. A black Suburban and a shiny red truck were parked in her driveway. There wasn't room for her car, so she parked by the mailbox, wondering what the hell they were up to now. They must be in her house. *How dare they think they can make themselves at home!* Anger reddened her cheeks as she clipped up the walk ready to tear more than one head off of someone's shoulders.

As she reached for the screen door, she spied both of them relaxing in her living room. The door slammed against the side of the house, and Mr. Pibbs went scuttling out of the way as she stomped into the room.

"What the hell are you two doing here?" Her delicate brows slanted over blazing green eyes as she pointed to the door. "Out! Both of you. Now!"

One man sent the other a rushed look and rose from where he sat. The other followed him up silently. "Lucy. It's nice to see you."

"Well, it's not nice to see you—either of you! I'll thank you to leave." Her foot tapped out a beat on the shiny hardwood floor as she tried to figure out who was who. In the hotel room, it had been easy. They had each been assigned a room and each was naked, one with a tiny scar on his breast.

Now, one took three steps and stood beside his brother. Neither had even the sense to look sheepish as they stared at her.

Lucy could have sworn she was looking at only one man who stood before a mirror with his reflection staring back. The only difference was the clothes they wore — *and the way they make love...* She shook the mental images her thought provoked and crossed her arms. "Should I call the cops and tell them you've broken into my house?"

"The door was wide open, Lucy. How many times have I told you to lock it when you leave?"

She finally knew which man was Matt. *Okay, Luce — blue shirt is Matt, red is Jake.*

Matt spoke again. "Would you please sit down and talk to us? We have something we want to say to you."

Get rid of them! her brain screamed silently. This could be nothing but trouble — double trouble.

"I have nothing to say to you."

"That's not what Matt asked you to do. He asked you to listen for a minute."

It struck her again how much the two sounded alike when her gaze snapped back to Jake. "What can you say that I haven't already heard? You're just spinning your wheels here." It took Lucy all the strength she could muster not to jump into one of the men's arms. She didn't care which one; she just wanted to hold someone that she loved. But which one would it be? She'd fallen crazy in love with Matt, but somehow Jake had wormed his way into her heart too. She was infinitely thankful she would never have to make the decision.

Matt reached out and grasped her hand.

His touch sent an electric shock through her system.

"Please come to the kitchen and sit down. Give us ten minutes and then we'll leave if you want us to."

Lucy snatched her hand from his grip, lifted her chin with a flick of her long hair, and headed out of the living room. *I must be out of my mind. I should send them both packing…*

Matt and Jake eyed her huffy departure, and then sent one another a look of courage as they moved to follow her to the other room. When they reached the kitchen, Lucy was already perched nervously on a chair with her hands clasped before her on the table. They seated themselves quietly.

Suddenly, she jumped up, grabbed the timer off of the stove ledge, and returned to her chair. After setting the dial, she slammed the timer down hard in the center of the table. "You've got ten minutes tops and then you're out of here." Her mouth snapped shut as she waited with a pounding heart. She couldn't figure out what they were up to.

"All right," the blue shirted Matt started, "first, we'd like to apologize to you once more for what we did. It was horribly wrong for us to put you in that position. We also wanted you to know that we've never pulled something like that with any other woman."

"Lucky me to be the one you decided to pick on."

"You're taking up our ten minutes, Lucy. I'd appreciate it if you'd keep your mouth shut."

Her mouth dropped open at his audacity before she snapped her lips together again and tossed her chin upward.

"I have something I want to say to you, and then Jake will say what he needs to say." Matt reached forward and forced her fingers to open so he could take her hand in his. He brushed his thumb softly across the center of her smooth palm.

Lucy ignored the instant thrill of touching him again.

"It's been a long three weeks not having you in my life." He saw her blink quickly and wondered about it before continuing. *Does she feel the same?* "I've never met anyone else like you. You make me laugh with your hilarious antics. Your beauty isn't only on the outside, because believe me, you are the sexiest woman I've ever met, and I miss you terribly. You've got a big heart that just bursts to love someone, and I want that someone to continue to be me." Her hand jerked, but he refused to let her go. "Please, Lucy, take me back. Give me another chance. Let me show you how much I love you."

Lucy stared at him, her heart melting with the emotions he stirred inside of her. But, across the table from him was another man that did the same thing to her. If Jake had spoken this plea, how would she choose? Just for the fact that she wouldn't be able to make a decision, Lucy hated the obvious outcome of this conversation. She would have to tell both of them goodbye and be miserable her entire life.

Her attention was drawn to Jake when he grasped her other hand and squeezed it gently. A soft smile preceded his apology. "I'm so sorry, Lucy, for everything I put you through. I should have never taken what you unknowingly offered that first time, because I not only hurt you in the end, but I took a huge chance of losing Matt's trust in me. Because of the connection he and I will always have, we've been able to put the past aside. I hope you will also. Lucy, I love you, too. It happened so quickly that it made my head spin. Lucy, take me back. Give me another chance. Let me show you how much I love you."

Lucy blinked once. And then she blinked again, followed by a quick shake of her head. Had she heard them right or was her brain morphing them together again? They had spoken the exact same words to her only seconds apart—and only inches apart from where they sat on either side of her. Now, both sat with wide matching grins across their face, not the least bit concerned about what the other had declared.

She blinked again and remained totally speechless. She didn't have a clue how to answer them.

A rumble of a chuckle was heard just before Matt glanced across to Jake. "Well, brother of mine, I think she's finally ready to listen."

Jake nodded. "I think you're right. Why don't you continue, Matt? I don't think you'll get any interruptions."

Lucy glanced from one to the other. Their voices were like an echo across her kitchen table.

"Marry us, Lucy."

She shook off their hands, bounded from the table to put distance between them, tripped, and skidded across the floor on her butt.

Matt and Jake leapt from their chairs at the same time.

"Sit down!" Lucy bellowed as she scrambled to her feet and backed up a few steps while rubbing her sore ass. "Don't you *dare* move from those chairs!"

They scattered back to the table and took their seats again.

She shook her head to clear it and stared at Matt once more. "What did you just say?"

"I said, marry us."

"What!"

"He said, *marry us*. Both of us. We love you—you love us. What's so hard about the decision to say yes?" Jake looked like he thought it was the easiest choice in the world to make.

"Are you two crazy?"

"Yes, we are," it was the blue shirt talking now. "We're both crazy about you and we've figured out a solution to our problem."

Lucy wrapped her arms around her body to stop the instant shivers that overtook her. "You seem to forget that there's only one of me and two of you."

"We've got that figured out." Mr. Red Shirt smiled across at her.

Lucy rolled her eyes. "Just for shits and giggles, fill me in— I can't wait to hear your 'solution'."

Matt reached into his pocket and laid a shiny gold band in the middle of the table. Upon closer inspection from her vantage point across the room, Lucy spied the two twinkling diamonds that were inset on either side of a rather large emerald. "Jake and I had this engagement ring made especially for you. These two diamonds signify our love for you—one is from Jake and the other is from me. The emerald in the center is you—for your beautiful green eyes. See how the diamonds protect the emerald?"

Her complexion had gone so white that her freckles appeared as ink spots peppered across her nose. Her head shook slowly while never taking her gaze from the ring. "You're out of your mind. We can't get married—I mean all of us. That's against the law."

"We've discussed that." It was Jake talking now. "Matt and I have always shared everything that was important to us in this world. It's always been one for the other. We can read one another's mind and know what the other twin is going to say before it even comes out of his mouth. You were the first person or thing that ever affected that ability. You rattled us like nobody else has ever done. Do you know that we never left the hotel that day? Instead, we stayed up all night talking about you and how we felt about you. We discussed how we could figure out this three-way relationship we've found ourselves in."

It was the craziest thing she had ever heard. There could be no solution but to go their separate ways. It would never work—especially when they had mentioned marriage and an engagement ring sat winking at her from the center of the table. The idea was ludicrous.

She couldn't take her eyes from the sparkling jewels. "So...even if I were to agree to this insane idea and just for the hell of it *again*, how do you see this playing out?" She had to know.

"We see a man and a woman marrying." Matt leaned forward with hope in his eyes. "We see a twin brother living with them. The world doesn't have to know that the three sleep together in the same bed. Only those three people would know of the bond that exists between them."

"What!" came her strangled response. Her eyes bulged in their sockets.

The brothers signaled silently to each other, rose from the table, and approached Lucy. She backed up until the kitchen sink stopped any further progress, flipping her wary gaze from one to the other.

"What?" she squeaked out. Her palms found the cold metal of the stainless steel sink behind her.

Jake leaned forward, brushed his lips against hers, and nuzzled her neck. His breath warmed her ear, immediately sending a thrill down her spine. "We both want you. You said you had fallen in love with not only Matt, but also me." Her body responded to his nearness with a mind of its own. There was absolutely nothing she could do about it. "Sleep with us, Lucy. Let us show you some double love."

Her stomach tumbled as her eyes slammed shut. A ménage? She'd never even given it a thought. Lucy searched for the anger that had fueled her original plan to make them both pay for the trick they'd pulled. It was nowhere to be found.

Before she could at least agree to disagree, a hand slid down her stomach and rested between her legs. She knew it must be Matt's because one of Jake's hands rested on her shoulder and his other massaged one of her nipples through her shirt until it swelled in response. Soon, she couldn't tell whose hand belonged to whom as they gently traveled the slopes and valleys of her trembling body. Someone had a hand on her ass as another slid up beneath her shirt to unhook the clasp of her bra between her breasts. Lucy was in heaven as her eyes fluttered open.

Jake lifted her into his arms and waited to see if she would object. She simply lay in his embrace with a stunned look. He headed out of the kitchen. Matt followed after he stopped to pick up the ring and slip it into his front pocket.

Lucy's head fell backwards over Jake's muscular arm as he kissed the gentle swell of her breasts. They ascended the steps, three people ready to discover a new adventure in bed.

Chapter Seventeen: One, Two, Three...

Jake let her body slide down the firm length of his upper torso when they reached the bedroom. Before her feet touched the carpet, Matt was behind her, his erection pressing against her ass, with his arms wrapped around her and his hands caressing her breasts, building her excitement before her clothes had even left her body.

"Lift your arms," Jake whispered.

She wordlessly obeyed. He slid her open shirt upwards and over her wrists while Matt slid his hands to the front of her pants. He unsnapped the button and worked the zipper down as his lips nuzzled the back of her neck.

The erotic sensation of having two men touch her and strip her of her clothes heated Lucy's blood—especially when she quit fighting the love she felt for both of them. She remained in a building sensual fog when Matt's hands returned to her breasts. His hard body supported her from behind as Jake slid her pants down her legs. Her lacy panties followed.

Jake pulled Lucy close when Matt stepped back to undress. He kissed her as his hands followed the straight line of her back to her ass. He yearned to touch her intimately, but would wait until they had her on the bed. This night would be the first of many if Lucy decided to agree to their proposal. He and Matt needed to drive her over the edge of reason together.

Matt stepped close and slid his erection between her thighs to tease her as Jake quickly undressed. He backed away each time Lucy's body dipped backwards to capture his cock inside of her. Not yet...not until Jake was ready.

Together, they led her to the canopied bed. Lucy trembled with excitement as her bare skin was pressed against the cool satin of the bedspread. She had missed them so much—each one of them separately and the same. Now they were granting her the chance to love both of them. She stared at each as they lay down beside her—one to the left and one to the right. "I've never done this with two men. I don't know what to do."

"Don't do anything."

She didn't know who spoke.

The other man whispered from his side. "Let us love you. If you discover you want something, let us know.

Hands slid across her bare skin, leaving her yearning and wiggling between them. They brushed her breasts, tweaked her nipples, and massaged her legs to her feet and back up again. Lucy quivered in ecstasy as they heated her skin wherever they touched. At the exact same moment, the fingers of each man gently grasped her inner thighs and spread her legs across the surface of the bed. There was a dark head at each of her breasts, licking and sucking at her nipples as each swirled a hand across the taut skin of her belly and down through her pubic hair.

"Oh my God…" Lucy whimpered into the semi-dark room. Her hips surged upwards to let the brothers know what she needed.

Matt and Jake eyed one another across her body as their hands found the inside of her thighs. They nodded silently and each inserted a finger into her pussy. Lucy's legs lurched wider as she pumped against the hands that brought her so much pleasure. This is how the brothers had agreed that Lucy would orgasm the first time the three of them were together; each with equal and twin participation; each simultaneously making her writhe with pleasure. This first time, no one man would have less of her; no one man would have more.

Lucy groaned as they slid in and out of her, each taking their turn to swirl around her swollen clit with a wet finger. She humped wildly against their hands. When she lifted her hips to clasp them tightly inside of her, both men buried their finger and let her orgasm pulse around them. To them, this was more of a union of the three of them than any wedding could ever bring them. They both shared Lucy's body equally at this moment.

Lucy's hips jumped once more when someone flicked her clit gently, and then she settled to the surface of the bed, her legs splayed, her loves kissing her breasts while their fingers rested inside her pussy. It was going to be a beautiful night.

She wasn't quite sure which man was Matt and which man was Jake. What she was sure of was that by the end of the night, she would be able to tell the difference by their own unique ways of making love. And if she wasn't certain even then? She would simply look for the scar.

"We both made you come. We wanted to share you equally this first time. I love you, Lucy."

"I love you, too." The masculine whisper came from the opposite side.

Lucy trembled between their shared heat. She looked from one to the other. God help her, she loved both of them and they had discovered a way for all of them to be together. The thought of having two gorgeous men who loved her in her bed every night caused a smile to break across her mouth. "I can't believe I'm going to say this, but yes! Yes, this *might* work."

Matt smiled. "You don't sound totally convinced." His palm rested between her legs.

Lucy gulped when Jake circled her nipple with his tongue. "I'm...I'm convinced that I never want either of you to leave, but..."

"But nothing, Luce. By the time we're done with you, you'll be ready to order a wedding gown. It'll work—we've got all the details figured out. Just let us worry about it." Matt ran his fingertip through her slick crease, causing her to rock against his hand.

She moaned with a smile and spread her legs further. "Convince me then..."

Jake crawled between her legs, flattened to his stomach, and stared at her glistening pussy. Using his thumbs, he tenderly opened her wider as he licked through her wet folds. "Mmmm—you taste so good. God, I've missed you." He began his assault with another long lick, ending the tortuous path he'd created by clasping his seeking lips around her clit. Another loud groan was heard from Lucy's mouth as she surged forward.

Matt rose to his knees and offered his penis to her waiting lips. Lucy angled her head and delicately licked the salty tip. As much as she wanted to take him completely into her mouth, she refused to leave Jake's lapping tongue. "Come closer," she whispered up to him. Matt hurried to straddle her chest and dipped his cock past her lips. She devoured it excitedly as he thrust into her throat and she thrust her pussy against Jake's mouth. Tongues swirled and bodies trembled.

Lucy sucked wildly, her excitement building as Jake rammed his finger into her and flattened his tongue against her clitoris. Liquid dripped from her as she jerked around his fingers, the waves of her second orgasm sending sparks through her body. She moaned loudly as she drew Matt's penis further into her mouth, and then whimpered softly as the pulses slowed through her vagina.

Matt swung his leg over her, lay back and pulled her body on top of him as Jake helped to roll Lucy to her stomach. Her breasts flattened against the wiry hair of one lover's chest as the other yanked her legs wide and around his brother to expose her pussy.

Rising to his knees, Jake guided his cock between the soft fur of her lips, and slid deeply into her. He filled her and began to pump, loving the sight of her firm ass and the sight of Matt's hands gliding over the soft skin of her back. A feeling of completeness after missing her so intensely washed over him as he throbbed inside of Lucy. He pumped harder while Matt's hands slipped to her shoulders to hold her body in place. Jake came unexpectedly. A small part of his brain had screamed for him to pull out, but he couldn't help himself. Just the feel of her tight lips around his cock had driven him crazy with lust. Lucy backed up and down his shriveling erection to find her own release again, but it was too late.

He rolled from his knees to lie on his side, his breaths jagged and harsh.

Lucy lifted her mouth from Matt's searching lips and stared at Jake with pleading eyes. "I need to come—I'm almost there again..."

He smiled with eyes twinkling back. "Aren't you about the luckiest woman in the world to have someone ready to fill that need."

Matt gently rolled her body to the mattress. She landed between the two men on the bed. Just as quickly, he was probing against her wetness with his hard erection, and slipped inside her.

Lucy's world spun as Matt brought her body back to near orgasm once more.

To her side, Jake rested his head above a bent elbow and fondled her breasts, watching and waiting as she brought her knees up and wrapped her legs around his brothers thrusting hips.

Having two men who looked exactly alike, one beside her, his fingers tugging at her nipples, and another with a thick cock that knocked against her womb, was unimaginable in the past. The experience was almost surreal, but as her body arched to suck at Matt's erection with an explosion of joy, Lucy realized that the two of them would be in her world forever.

As she floated back to the reality of Matt and Jake's protective heat surrounding her from all sides as they lay in the quiet, a calming smile of pure happiness and love curved her mouth upward. She would never have to send them away. She would never have to make the horrible choice of selecting one man above the other. They loved her enough to share her forever, and she would spend the rest of her life never having to worry about being alone again. Time passed as Lucy, Matt, and Jake stared into the darkening room, totally engulfed with the passion of simply being together again.

Both men glanced in her direction when she giggled between them. Lucy shot up suddenly and looked from one to the other with a huge smile. She sat cross-legged, her hair tumbling around her shoulders. "Would you two tell me how you have this figured out?"

Jake stretched his long torso and placed his hands beneath his head against the pillow. "Go ahead, Matt."

Matt rolled to his side and leaned on his elbow. His finger curled in a wavy lock. Pulling it close, he breathed in the clean, fresh scent of her hair. "First, I want you to know we didn't toss a coin to see who would officially marry you. I loved you first, Lucy. And you loved me. If we had never pulled the switch on you, I still would have asked you to spend the rest of your life with me."

Her heart swelled with his words, but she remained silent.

"Jake will be our best man and no one will be the wiser. Only the three of us will know that it will also be an unofficial union between you and him. Jake and I have lived together most of our lives. We've shared everything up to this point. After the wedding, you and I become a couple who has a brother living with us."

Jake took her hand and kissed her knuckles gently. "Except for some personal belongings and our vehicles, everything we own is under both our names. We want to include your name alongside ours. If you decide to do this, you'll be a very wealthy woman. Think about it, Lucy. We don't have a problem with this. I think we showed you that over the last hour."

Matt shuffled the pillow behind his back and sat up against the headboard. He grasped her other hand. "We both love you. You're the nuttiest redhead we've ever met—you make our lives complete. You're special, Lucy—so why shouldn't you accept our proposal? It's a special situation."

Jake's glittering blue eyes smiled. "Just think. Whenever you need to be fulfilled, one of us will be at your side—or both of us." His hand slid up her leg. A single finger played about the moist folds of her body. "Marry us."

Matt leaned forward and nuzzled her neck. "Marry me, Lucy. Marry us. You'll never be sorry."

Her heart hammered in her chest. Their idea was totally insane, unheard of. Yet, as she gazed at the two of them, her mind finally cleared. Why not? Officially, her and Matt's union would be legal and she would have these two men in her life forever.

A smile of acceptance widened across her face. "Yes...yes! I can't believe I'm saying this, but yes! I want both of you." She burst into tears a second later.

Matt and Jake stiffened with apprehension.

"What's wrong?" they said in unison.

"Nothing—"

"Then why are you crying?" Their words bounced off of her at the same time.

She grabbed the edges of the sheet and wiped her eyes. "Because I'm so damn happy. So damned doubly happy!

Chapter Eighteen: The Honeymoon

Lucy strolled across the deck of the private yacht and sank into a lounge chair. Other than the minimal crew to take care of them, it was only she, Jake, and Matt aboard.

She sighed with contentment even as a shiver of anticipation raced up her spine. Lifting her hand to let the sun glint off her wedding ring, she inspected the double diamonds and single emerald that were now surrounded by a swirling wedding band of gold. After flying to Florida to meet their parents, the three of them had flown to the Mediterranean yesterday. She and Matt had been married early this very afternoon by a Justice of the Peace who came on board with only Jake by their side. It was a beautiful ceremony of love as the cruiser bobbed gently in the afternoon sun. She had lovingly hung her wedding dress in a cabinet below and now had changed to a tiny string bikini.

A giggle bubbled in her throat as she hugged herself thinking about how the two had stared at her with lust blazing in her eyes when she came topside. Matt and Jake were both busy with details as they began their two-week long honeymoon, sailing from port to port. She had come up the stairs only moments earlier, the small bikini barely covering her body, and stretched contentedly before leaning against the railing with her head back and her breasts bulging over a skimpy piece of material. It was all the two of them could do to keep their attention on what the captain spoke to them about. She had felt their hot gazes devouring her as she strolled away.

Since the night they proposed to her, Lucy had declared her body off limits until the ceremony took place—something she felt would help build the excitement until they were an official trio. It had driven both men to the edge of reason, but no more so than the emotions that ran through her now. It had been two months since they made love together. That would change soon.

Despite the heat, the hair raised on her arms. She leaned back and closed her eyes, waiting for them to come for her.

Fifteen minutes passed as she floated in and out of a contented slumber, before the bright light from the sun suddenly dimmed. Lucy's eyes fluttered open to discover what blocked the sun's rays. Matt and Jake surrounded her lounge.

"Hi," she giggled, and then ran her hands over her breasts.

Lust again shot from their eyes. Jake nodded his head, turned, and disappeared through the portal leading to their cabin. Matt bent, lifted her into his arms, and followed his brother.

"Where are we going?" Lucy had to ask even though she knew.

"We've waited long enough for you."

His head dipped as he kissed her. "Congratulations, Mrs. Diamond. You've managed to turn the two of us into you."

She laughed against his mouth. "And what do you mean by that?"

"Hah! Like you don't know. We've fumbled around the last two months, trying to find things to occupy ourselves with because you decided there would be no sex until you had us legally tied to you! I haven't seen you break a glass or fall on your ass in all that time. Jake has six dents in his new truck from carelessness, and I haven't had a good night's sleep in over a month."

Lucy simply giggled louder at his comment and grasped his neck tighter as he retreated through the portal and down the steps.

"We plan to fix that shortly. Consider that a fact."

Her finger trailed across his chest. "You're not going to wait until it gets dark and we can light candles?"

"Fuck the candles. I'm not waiting a minute longer."

Lucy burst out laughing, and then struggled to control her breathing when he entered the cabin. Jake was just turning down the huge bed. The curtains were already closed. He was buck-assed naked with an erection standing tall between his legs. As she slid down Matt's body, she felt his bulge against her thigh.

Lucy strolled to the middle of the room. When she turned, Matt had kicked off his swimming trunks and moved to stand near his brother.

She bestowed each with a smoldering glance as she unclasped her bikini top and let her breasts spill forward. Lucy didn't have to look down. She could feel her nipples were puckered into hard darts. Slowly, she worked her thong down her trim, tanned legs and stood naked before them. Her blood raced through her veins at the thought of what was to transpire over the next few hours. The two-month wait was harder on her, she suspected, than it was on her two lovers, but she would never admit to it.

Crossing the thick carpet to stand before them, she reached out and took each of their penises in her palms. A hiss of excitement left both men's mouths. Lucy leaned forward and kissed Matt first. "I love you." Then she turned to Jake and brushed her lips across his waiting mouth. "I love you, too."

She dropped gracefully to her knees and kneeled before them. "I will love you both for as long as I live…"

As she stroked Jake, Lucy slid her tongue around the tip of Matt's cock, nibbling and sucking gently, and then she treated Jake with the same.

Their matching chests ballooned with excitement as she continued to caress them and alternately suck on their cocks. When neither could take her adoring licks any longer, she was carried to the bed and laid gently onto the center.

Jake lay beside her, collected her into his embrace, and ran his tongue around the perimeter of her mouth before searching for something more. Lucy danced her tongue against his, acutely aware that Matt stroked her thighs as he positioned himself between her legs.

Her body hummed when he pressed her legs wider and kissed her pussy. Lucy's honeymoon had begun.

She moaned against Jake's lips when his hand found a swollen breast. He teased her nipples by rolling them between his fingers and continued to swirl his tongue in her mouth. Groaning louder, her body responded with thrusts of her hips as Matt continued to lick her wet slit. His fingers played inside and back out of her hole.

When she bucked forward with waves of heat racing through her groin, Jake squeezed her breasts and quickly moved his lips to a hard nipple, drawing it deeply into his mouth until her body calmed and the small pants from her mouth evened to a steady pace. Her first orgasm was sweet, sensual, and an indication of what was to come.

Lucy struggled to a sitting position with the help of Jake's hands and searched the faces of the men she loved. She needed something more—something she had thought about over the past two months. She needed to make this first day special. Reaching for Matt, her hands urged him closer. "Come here, Matt. I want you to lie down."

He crawled nearer, wondering what she had planned. One of her hands rested against his cheek and the other found Jake's fingers. Their erections were stiff and hard with anticipation as her gaze moved over them.

"I want to do something different. I want to show you both how much I love you. I think I can do that by loving you at the same time. I want one of you in my pussy and one of you in my ass. I've been thinking about this since the first night we were together."

"You never cease to amaze me," Matt responded from where he lay on the bed.

"Or me," Jake breathed out excitedly. "Just how do you suggest we do this?"

Lucy lifted her leg and straddled Matt. "Like this," she smiled wickedly. Jake watched her slide down his brother's hard length. Her head fell back, and her lids closed momentarily as she enjoyed being filled for the first time in a long time.

The air whistled from Matt's lungs as his hips moved slowly, relishing the feel of her hot pussy wrapped around his shaft.

Her body arched slightly as she sat impaled on top of him.

"Oh, God, it's been too long." Her heavy lidded gaze moved to Jake who stroked his penis as he watched them. "Come join us," she smiled. "I need both of you in me—I want my double diamonds to make me shudder with pleasure."

Jake moved behind her. Placing his hand on her back, he gently forced her to lie forward across Matt's chest. Lucy captured her first love's mouth with hers as she waited for Jake to penetrate her. They had never tried this, but just the thought of one man's cock in her pussy and the other in her ass had her blood on fire.

Jake reached for the lubricant that lay on the bed stand, moistened his cock, and then traced his finger around her soft anus, licking his lips as he inserted the tip of one gelled finger to ready her. A deep groan came from Lucy's throat when he shoved it in further.

"Hurry, Jake!" Her hips were moving now, her pussy sliding up and down Matt's cock.

He straddled Matt's legs and slowly guided his cock into Lucy's rectum. He didn't want to hurt her with his brother already fucking her in the pussy. "Are you okay, Luce?" God, he hoped so, because he didn't know how he was going to back out if she asked him to stop.

Lucy barely heard him. The feel of being completely filled by the two men she loved so deeply, of being in one of the most intimate of positions ever, made her weak with desire. "Ohhh…" she moaned. "Fuck me, Matt—Fuck me, Jake."

Her body began to move at a faster tempo, showing them, guiding them to what she wanted, what she had to have.

Lucy began to slam down Matt's shaft as Jake bounced against her ass from behind. Her eyes opened and she stared at the ring on her finger glinting in a ray of sunlight that had snuck its way through the curtains.

An emerald between two diamonds...the heat began to build in her womb.

"Fuck me harder!"

The feeling was like nothing she'd ever experienced. She fucked them separately but together. Hot shards spiked through her lower body, building hotter and hotter as she rocked against them.

Matt sucked at her lips as he thrust upward.

Jake nipped at her back as he plunged inward.

Her two men fucked themselves into a crescendo...her two double diamonds.

At the same time, their strokes jerked forcibly forward, only to hesitate for an instant before slamming back into her again.

"Now!" Lucy screamed as a tremendous orgasm spasmed through her vagina, sending rivers of molten lava in one direction to her rectum and the other to her swaying breasts. Her entire body was engulfed with blazing heat from head from to toe. The breath was sucked from her lungs, her heart raced, and still the flames continued. Her body shuddered with not only the physical sensation of their thick cocks filling her, but with the emotional awareness of the two men she loved deeply.

Matt jerked against her, his cum spilling into her.

Jake followed with the same motion only seconds later, spilling hot liquid into her ass.

"I love you!" Lucy sobbed out as she continued to shudder around their hard lengths.

The ring sparkled against her finger; the emerald forever protected by the double diamonds.

Also in eBook from Ellora's Cave Publishing, Inc.

www.ellorascave.com

An Excerpt From:

PAYTON'S PASSION

"Are you really going to make us put on costumes?"

"You're damned right. Look at this." She held up a cotton gauze, see-through robe. "I want to see what your reaction is when I put this on!"

"Ooo, my harem girl. I'll be right back." He scooted behind the screen. "This better not be a joke, Payton. When I come out, you'd better have that outfit on."

She was already pulling her shirt over her head and heading for another corner of the room that was screened off.

A few minutes later, Andy stepped from behind the privacy panel. He wore a long flowing sheik's robe, complete with headgear. "I can't believe I'm doing this." He glanced around until he saw her clothes hanging over the top of her dressing area. "Payton, you almost done back there?"

A rustle of material preceded her as she floated into the room.

A rush of air whistled across Andy's teeth as he stared at his wife who had suddenly transformed herself into an Arabic concubine.

She was stunning to say the least.

A silver band wrapped around her head just above her eyebrows. Matching silver hoops bounced from her delicate earlobes as she raised her chin a notch to let him view the sweet length of her slender neck. Payton had pulled her long blonde tresses into a swirling mass at the top of her head. Springing curls draped their way around her neck, making him want to reach out to feel their softness.

That need, however, didn't match the desire he felt to gather her body into his arms to assure himself she was real. The filmy gauze floated along the sensuous curves of her breasts and thighs. Her pubic hair was barely discernable beneath the white threads, and Andy knew the joy he would find just beneath the curly mound.

Payton's nipples immediately hardened when his heated gaze raked her from head to toe. Slender hands reached up to caress the muted pink nipples draped by the material. She brushed her fingers down past her hips, around to the apex of her legs, and back up to rest gently on her trim hips. "Do you like what you see?"

He nodded.

"It opens in the front. In just one little flick of your finger, you could be inside my robe."

He took a step forward, but she raised a palm to halt his approach.

"Not yet, though. I love the feel of this material against my skin. I want to stay dressed for awhile."

"You have nothing underneath it. It's pretty clear to me that all I'd have to do is lift up the hem and you'd be mine before you knew it. I don't need to open anything. I've got a hard-on that hurts just looking at you."

A satisfied smile turned up the corners of Payton's mouth. That's exactly the reaction she had gone for, but she was going to make him wait. Like he said; the anticipation was half the game.

Payton sank to a pillow and patted the one across from her. "Here, sit so we can talk. I took a quick glimpse at the manual. We're supposed to communicate orally first."

"You want *oral communication*? I'll give you *oral communication*."

"That's not what I'm talking about and you know it. But...I'll remember you said that."

His jaw clenched, but he sat across from her as ordered.

"You look handsome in that robe, Andy. With your dark masculine physique, you could easily be sitting in an Arabian tent with a camel waiting for you outside."

"I feel a little silly."

"Don't—the sight of you turns me on. It helps my fantasy along."

"Which is...?"

"In due time," she answered cheekily. "My manual gave me a few ideas, but it also asked me a question." The smile left her face as she reflected inwardly for a moment. "I'm supposed to discuss with you the exact moment when I knew you and I would make a life together—when I was absolutely sure you would always be by my side."

"Did something come to mind?"

"Yes—it did."

"And…?"

Payton leaned back against a larger pillow and stared at him. A soft, mellow love rested in her blue gaze. "At the hospital—after Tyler was born."

Surprise widened her husband's eyes. "I thought you'd pick some great sexual experience—like maybe a time when we connected more so than any other."

Her head shook slightly. "I heard you in the hallway talking to my parents after he was born. You're words warmed me and gave me security like nothing else ever has."

"I can't remember what you're talking about." He tilted his head, then shook it with uncertainty furrowing his brow. "A conversation with your parents?"

"Yes. I don't think I was listening to the first part of the discussion. I did hear, however, your voice charged with emotion—that's what caught my attention."

As she spoke, an emotion of protectiveness warmed his blood. He was beginning to remember now exactly what she was talking about.

"What did they say to you that made you respond the way you did? You told them that they were making a huge mistake."

Andy squirmed. It was a conversation he had buried, planning to never let Payton know how her parents were ready to throw her away. If it weren't for him, they would have walked out of her life after the wedding. But, numerous calls when Payton wasn't around had guilted them into visiting occasionally or to at least call her on the phone to see how the pregnancy was progressing.

"Andy? Was the mistake that...they had decided they didn't want me in their life anymore?" A lump formed in her throat. Payton was amazed that after all the wonderful years she created with Andy, her family still had the power to break her heart. She hadn't seen her brothers since the day of her wedding. "My parents aren't the kind of grandparents I thought they would be. The kids don't even know them. What did you tell them?"

He studied her beautiful features. Did he really want all this brought up now? It might put a damper on their weekend — especially when they'd had so much fun thus far. But, wasn't communication the reason they were here? "All right. I told them they were fools to put such stock in one mistake. I asked them to think about all the years you worked hard alongside them — to think about your high academic honors and how you never caused them an ounce of trouble your entire life. Those things had to count for something. I also told them you were still their daughter, even though you were beginning your own family."

"And why did you tell them that?"

Andy sighed. "Because they said that you and Tyler were now my responsibility. Their duty was done and they felt they failed. It was easier for them in their square little world to just dismiss you and go about their days."

An instant tear trickled its way down Payton's cheek.

"Christ, Payton. Talking about this does nothing but upset you. Fuck them. You've got me, the kids, and my parents, who love you deeply. Why are we talking about this anyway?"

She dabbed at the tear with the gauzy hem of her robe, then took a deep breath. "Because of the manual and its question to me." She leaned forward, held out her arm, and waited for his fingers to touch hers. It always amazed her how his warm touch seemed to make things right when her world became rocky. "I didn't hear that entire conversation that night. What I did hear was you speaking with love and emotion in your voice. You stated how much you loved me and, no matter what, you would never leave my side—that Tyler wasn't a burden or a mistake—that he was your son. You said you'd die for both of us before letting anything hurt us again."

"I meant it. You're my life, Payton. Love isn't even a big enough word to explain how I feel about you."

Suddenly, the weight of her parents' refusal to be a part of her life anymore lifted from her shoulders. Andy was completely right. She hadn't done anything to deserve their complete dismissal. What she had now, most women would die for.

To hell with them. Andy was her life now.

Payton rose and pulled Andy up with her. "You know, Mr. Sheik, all of a sudden I'm rather horny. I think I need to do something about that." Her gaze flitted about the room, and then returned to his slightly whiskered face. "Want to hear my fantasy?"

"Want to hear mine?" His eyes bored through the gauzy material.

"Later. I'm first. Let's see," she pondered as she urged him across the room. "Normally, a sheik is in charge of his kingdom. But, I'm the smart, intimidating woman that has overtaken the empire that the overbearing sheik has created. It's all mine now—and you have become my slave." Her slender hands shoved him against the padded wall.

Andy smiled. "If I overtake you right now, I suppose your guards will take me down and make me pay for it?" He enjoyed the scenario she created and would play along.

"Oh, yes. You would be beaten and thrown into the dungeon. But," her finger traced a pattern across his chest, "I've decided that you would be better as a love slave rather than sending you to the fields to work out your days in the hot sun."

"I didn't know deserts had fields."

She grinned at his smart-assed comment. "It's my fantasy. I can have anything I want—and I think I want you."

Before he knew it, she grabbed his wrist, dragged his arm upward, and linked a handcuff around it. "If you fight me, remember the guards will be here instantly. You might not get to experience what the queen has decided." She clicked the handcuff shut.

Andy's breaths became heavier. "Your wish is my command."

"Lift your other arm up so that it can be bound."

He did and was rewarded with another click of the opposite handcuff.

The material of his robe rested over his erection. Payton eyed the area and whisked her fingers across it. "I see that you are a fine specimen. Big, long, and hard. Hmmmm. Remember, if you come too soon, I'll have you returned to the fields, never to have a woman interested in you again." She sank to her knees. "Now spread your feet wide enough so I can secure your ankles."

Andy spread his stance. Payton quickly wrapped the ankle ties around him and made certain they were fastened. Her sheik was totally immobilized. Rising to her feet, she smiled up at him. Andy licked his lips. Being completely at her disposal caused his cock to throb. He wondered what she had planned.

Payton dragged a three-tier stool closer to the wall where Andy was chained, and then returned to the chest. Withdrawing a soft feather whip, she turned to face him. Her head tipped to the side as she studied his body clamped to the wall.

"You are not to say a word unless spoken to. Only then, can you utter anything. If you do, I might have to use my whip on you. You are just a man with no power now. Only I have the power."

Andy was never so excited in his life.

She strolled across to him, reached out and caressed his balls gently through the silken material. The intake of his breath echoed in the room, but he remained silent.

"Very good. You obey rather well. We'll see how long it lasts. Nod your head if you're comfortable." A quick nod assured her that her sheik was at ease with the position he was in.

Dragging the wide stepstool closer, Payton placed it before him. A quick kick of her satin slippers and she was barefoot. She stepped regally up the three tiers. Her chest was eye-level with Andy's face.

He watched her closely, his eyes dark with lust.

Reaching a hand ever so slowly into the front of her gown, Payton massaged her breast before pushing aside the material to expose it to his view.

"I love having my nipples sucked, and I've decided to see if you are worthy enough to continue on with my desires. If not, I'll find someone else to take your place."

She leaned slightly forward and whisked her nipple past his open mouth, and then quickly pulled back just out of his reach.

A low growl erupted from Andy's throat.

In response, Payton undid the clasps at the top of her shoulders. The gauzy bodice material drifted down to the sash tied around her waist. She fondled both exposed breasts that were mere inches from his mouth. "I don't know what I was thinking. How could I tell if you're good at sucking nipples when I only offered you one?" Raising her arms, she placed her hands against the padded wall above his head and brushed the tips of her breasts across his face.

Andy snatched out at a wayward nipple with his mouth, captured it between his lips, and sucked with force.

Hot streams of excitement raced through Payton's blood. The idea that he would do anything she asked fueled her on. Pulling back to break the suction, she offered her opposite breast. Andy immediately imprisoned the hard dart of her nipple and swirled his tongue around its perimeter.

Payton grasped her breast and forced it tighter against his mouth. Her breaths were tiny pants as she fought to maintain control. "You're very good. That's it. Suck it hard. Just think what it would be like if you were putting your finger in me at the same time."

Andy groaned behind his closed eyelids and sucked harder. The muscles of his forearms clenched as he tried to pull free. He wanted to fuck her so bad that he ached. The nipple was pulled from his mouth. He eyed the breasts that hung just out of his reach with longing.

Payton's blue eyes danced about the room again. She scrambled off the footstool, hauled it out of the way, found one that wasn't as tall, and dragged it back before him. As she stepped up on her new perch, her gaze swept the length of him. "I don't think I like the fact that you're still dressed. Wearing that outfit makes you still look like the king in charge—and you're not. You're nothing but my slave." She reached up and yanked the front open in one fluid motion. The muscles of his chest quivered when she ran her hands across his breasts. Quick fingers untied the sash at his waist. Andy's erection was hard and dripping pre-ejaculate. Payton was quick to stuff the ends of the robe between her husband's body and the wall to keep the material out of the way.

She reached down, pressed her palms against the inside of his spread knees, and traveled a sensuous path up his inner thighs, swirled her hands around his balls, and then took his cock in her hands. Andy arched forward and expelled the breath he held.

"You can answer me now. You like this, don't you."

"Christ, Payton, you're driving me crazy…"

"That's all. You can be quiet now."

His mouth snapped shut.

Continuing to slowly stroke his hard length, she looked up at him. Andy's stare bore into her. "You've been so good, that we might continue this…" she squeezed her fingers around his cock, applied slight pressure, and then pulled her hands away from him, "…or not."

She watched his eyelids drop when he inhaled deeply.

"Or we could try this."

His eyes snapped back open when she dropped to her knees.

About the author:

Ruby Storm was born and raised in Minnesota and has lived there her entire life. Spending time in the outdoors is something she still enjoys immensely, whether it be camping or working in her garden.

Being an avid reader and relishing her state's history is what prompted her to begin writing seven years ago. She has published the first two novels of a trilogy for another publishing company and is finishing up the third installment. Ruby and her husband of twenty-eight years (also her high school sweetheart) have three children and many friends and family who have supported her desire to write. Being captivated with it, she doesn't plan to stop any time soon. She also plans to have a long and sizzling relationship with Ellora's Cave.

Ruby welcomes mail from readers. You can write to her c/o Ellora's Cave Publishing at 1337 Commerce Drive, Suite 13, Stow OH 44224.

Also by Ruby Storm:

Payton's Passion
Virgin Queen

Why an electronic book?

We live in the Information Age—an exciting time in the history of human civilization in which technology rules supreme and continues to progress in leaps and bounds every minute of every hour of every day. For a multitude of reasons, more and more avid literary fans are opting to purchase e-books instead of paperbacks. The question to those not yet initiated to the world of electronic reading is simply: *why?*

1. *Price.* An electronic title at Ellora's Cave Publishing runs anywhere from 40-75% less than the cover price of the <u>exact same title</u> in paperback format. Why? Cold mathematics. It is less expensive to publish an e-book than it is to publish a paperback, so the savings are passed along to the consumer.

2. *Space.* Running out of room to house your paperback books? That is one worry you will never have with electronic novels. For a low one-time cost, you can purchase a handheld computer designed specifically for e-reading purposes. Many e-readers are larger than the average handheld, giving you plenty of screen room. Better yet, hundreds of titles can be stored within your new library—a single microchip. (Please note that Ellora's Cave does not endorse any specific brands. You can check our website at www.ellorascave.com for customer

recommendations we make available to new consumers.)

3. *Mobility.* Because your new library now consists of only a microchip, your entire cache of books can be taken with you wherever you go.

4. *Personal preferences are accounted for.* Are the words you are currently reading too small? Too large? Too...**ANNOYING**? Paperback books cannot be modified according to personal preferences, but e-books can.

5. *Innovation.* The way you read a book is not the only advancement the Information Age has gifted the literary community with. There is also the factor of what you can read. Ellora's Cave Publishing will be introducing a new line of interactive titles that are available in e-book format only.

6. *Instant gratification.* Is it the middle of the night and all the bookstores are closed? Are you tired of waiting days—sometimes weeks—for online and offline bookstores to ship the novels you bought? Ellora's Cave Publishing sells instantaneous downloads 24 hours a day, 7 days a week, 365 days a year. Our e-book delivery system is 100% automated, meaning your order is filled as soon as you pay for it.

Those are a few of the top reasons why electronic novels are displacing paperbacks for many an avid reader. As always, Ellora's Cave Publishing welcomes your questions and comments. We invite you to email us at service@ellorascave.com or write to us directly at: 1337 Commerce Drive, Suite 13, Stow OH 44224.

Printed in the United States
24638LVS00003B/76-729